IN SEARCH OF
THE LONG-LOST
MAVERICK

IN SEARCH OF THE LONG-LOST MAVERICK

CHRISTINE RIMMER

MILLS & BOON

® and TM are trademarks owned and used by the
trademark owner and/or its licensee. Trademarks
marked with ® are registered with the United Kingdom
Patent Office and/or the Office for Harmonisation in the
Internal Market and in other countries.

First published in Great Britain 2020
by Mills & Boon, an imprint of HarperCollins*Publishers*
1 London Bridge Street, London, SE1 9GF

Large Print edition 2020

© 2019 Harlequin Books S.A.

Special thanks and acknowledgement
are given to Christine Rimmer for her contribution to the
Montana Mavericks: What Happened to Beatrix? series.

ISBN: 978-0-263-08914-1

MIX
Paper from
responsible sources
FSC
www.fsc.org   FSC® C007454

This book is produced from independently certified
FSC™ paper to ensure responsible forest management. For
more information visit www.harpercollins.co.uk/green.

Printed and bound in Great Britain
by CPI Group (UK) Ltd, Croydon, CR0 4YY

For Callie Brazzell and her cat, Fury. Fury was found beside the dumpster at Zaxby's Chicken and is the inspiration for the sweet, wild-eyed black rescue kitten, Homer, in this story.
As all you Montana Mavericks fans have probably already guessed, Homer the kitten is named after eccentric moonshine-making Homer Gilmore, who has been delighting Montana Mavericks readers for many years now.

Prologue

Melanie Driscoll let out a shriek of dismay as the bride's bouquet came flying right at her. It hit her in the face. She put up both hands just in time to catch it before it dropped to the grass.

"Lucky girl!" cried a woman right behind her.

"No fair!" whined someone to her left. "I *never* catch the bouquet."

"Mel! You go, girl!" shouted her high school friend, Sarah Turner Crawford.

Mel blinked down at the gorgeous creation of sunflowers, asters, cornflowers and delphiniums and wondered what she was doing here at this relentlessly romantic outdoor wedding in Rust Creek Falls Park.

She shouldn't have come.

But Sarah had insisted. "Come on, Mel," Sarah had coaxed. "Believe me, I know exactly what you're going through." Sarah did know. She'd had some big troubles with men in the past. But now she was happily married to one of the five brothers of the groom. "It's going to be fun," Sarah had promised. "And you need to get out."

Fun. Right. Mel sneered at the bouquet.

"It's official," another of Mel's high-school friends announced with a giggle. "You're next!" Everybody started clapping.

Mel knew she should just roll with it. She should smile and pretend to be thrilled that her "turn" was coming right up.

But it wasn't coming up. Not a chance. Her life was a mess and a man was to blame. And as for smiling sweetly and pretending to be pleased as everyone applauded and hugged her and patted her on the back?

No way.

Mel tossed the damn thing back over her shoulder. She felt bitter satisfaction at the gasps and shouts of shocked surprise that followed.

Then a childish voice cried, "It's okay! I got it!"

Mel turned. Wren Crawford, the flower girl and daughter of the groom, came running toward her, ribbon-braided pig-tails bouncing, the giant bouquet of flowers clutched between her two small hands and her flower basket swaying on her arm. Wren skidded to a stop in front of Mel. Big blue eyes stared up at her accusingly. "You threw the bouquet away."

"Yes, I did."

"Don't you want to be the next bride?"

No, she did not. But the pretty little girl was only six or seven. Mel couldn't quite bring herself to say anything that might spoil Wren's innocent fantasies of love and happy-ever-after. Instead, she gentled her expression and answered softly, "You keep it. I don't have anyone special in my life right now."

One of the other single women muttered, "Well, if that kid is next, I'll be forty before *my* turn comes around."

Everybody laughed.

Except Wren and Mel. Frowning, the child continued to gaze up at her. "You came to the ranch with my aunt Sarah last week, didn't you?" Wren's branch of the Crawford family had moved to town the summer before. Her uncle Logan was now Sarah's husband.

"Yep. That was me. I'm your aunt Sarah's friend and my name's Mel."

"Mel, do you really want me to have this bouquet?"

"Yes, I do."

"Then I have something you are going to need." Wren turned and headed for a wooden bench several yards away.

Mel couldn't think of a single thing she might need from the little girl, but she trailed after her anyway—partly to get away from the crowd and partly out of curiosity.

"Sit down." Wren hopped up on one end of the bench, the organza skirt of her ivory lace dress fanning out around her like the petals of a delicate flower. Mel sat beside her. "Here." Wren held out the bouquet.

"No, thanks."

"Just for a minute. Please?"

Reluctantly, Mel took possession of the bouquet again. She watched, intrigued in spite of herself, as Wren folded back the swatch of ivory silk covering her flower basket and pulled out an old book. Of brown leather, it was studded with gemstones and stamped with a giant *A* on the front cover.

"It's a diary," Wren explained. "My uncles found it under a floorboard at the Ambling A." The Ambling A was the ranch where Wren lived with her dad and now her new stepmom, the bride, along with her grandpa and more than one of her dad's five brothers and their new brides. "Here." Wren held out the diary. "It's for you."

Mel's free hand seemed to open of its own accord. She looked down and the diary was firmly in her possession.

Wren hooked her flower basket over her arm again and held out her hands. "I'll take my flowers now." Still puzzled as to how, exactly, she'd allowed the child to give her the diary, Mel passed the flowers back. "Thank you," the pretty child said.

More than a little bewildered, Mel watched as Wren slid off the bench and started to walk away. "Wait!" She held out the old book. "You forgot your diary!"

Wren only smiled. "It's yours now."

"Huh? Wait. No…"

"Yes. It will bring you good luck in love. Just ask one of my uncles. They found the diary and they're all happily married now and so is my grandpa Max. And now, my daddy is married, too." Wren beamed, clearly thrilled that her father, Hunter Crawford, had tied the knot with Merry Matthews. "Ask my uncle Wilder," the little girl suggested. "Uncle Wilder will 'splain everything to you."

"But I—"

"He's right over there." Wren tipped her blond head in the direction of the uncle in question. "Bye." And off she went.

Mel jumped up to follow, but then changed her mind and headed for Wilder instead. If the child wouldn't take the old book, surely her uncle would. It looked like an antique and was probably quite valuable.

But Wilder Crawford shook his head when she tried to hand it over. "Mel, the diary is yours."

"No, it's not."

"You caught the bouquet and I'm thinking that means you're meant to be the next one to find love. The diary will help you with that."

Apparently, this branch of the Crawford family was a few screwdrivers short of a tool kit. "Wilder," she said patiently, "love has not been good to me and I have absolutely no interest in finding any more of it."

Wilder crossed his lean arms over his broad chest. "Open it."

"I just want you to—"

"Humor me. The diary. Open it."

She huffed out a hard breath to show her impatience with him and his adorable niece and the bride and the groom and just generally everyone and everything that had anything to do with love and forever and all that crap. Wilder was not impressed. He simply stood there, waiting for her to do what he'd asked her to.

"Fine." She opened the diary and Wren's uncle uncrossed his arms long enough to show her the place in the binding where a letter was hidden. A never-mailed letter, apparently. The wrinkled, dog-eared envelope was addressed to Winona Cobbs at a psychiatric facility in nearby Kalispell.

Mel was stunned. "*Our* Winona Cobbs?"

Wilder nodded. "Who else could it be? Rust Creek Falls is a very small town."

Mel knew Winona Cobbs well and was

fond of the old woman, who had shown up in town the summer before Mel lost both of her parents in a car accident. Wise and kindly, Winona was in her nineties now. Some considered her a little off in the head. Others believed she was psychic. Pretty much everyone had enjoyed her newspaper column, "Wisdom by Winona."

"It's a short letter," said Wilder. "Go ahead. Read it."

Mel tucked the diary under her arm, took the letter from the creased envelope and smoothed it out between her suddenly shaky hands.

My dearest Winona, please forgive me. But they say you will never get better. I promise you that your baby daughter is safe. She's alive! I wanted to raise her myself, but my parents forced me to have her placed for adoption. She is with good people—my parents don't know, but I have figured out who they are. Some-

day, I will find a way to bring her back to you.

Yours always,
Josiah

Mel refolded the letter. "Who's this Josiah person?"

"Josiah Abernathy. He was the son of the original owners of the Ambling A. He wrote the diary."

She had heard the old stories of the Abernathys. Years and years ago, they'd put the Ambling A up for sale and left town suddenly, never to be heard from again. "I know it seems unlikely that another Winona Cobbs lived in town all those years ago, but really, that has to be the case."

"Why?"

Mel stuck the letter in the envelope and eased it back into its hiding place in the binding of the old book. "Because *our* Winona has only lived in the area for the past six years." Mel held out the old diary for him to take. "I remember when she came to town." It was only a few months before Mel's parents died. "I met her that first summer she moved here. And then that fall, when my parents died and I came back from school to bury them, she was right there at my side, helping me any way she could, so kind and understanding and wise and loving. She made it possible for me to get through a very tough time."

"Everyone loves Winona," Wilder said gently. Then he shrugged. "And she could have lived here decades ago, moved away and then returned—and stop pushing that diary at me. It's yours now."

"But have you talked to Winona? Did you show her the letter?"

Wilder shoved his fingers in his hair and raked the thick, dark strands back off his forehead. "Look. My brothers and I have gone around and around about whether to approach Winona with this. But you know the situation. Winona's so old and she's been sick a lot lately. We just weren't sure if it was a good idea to go there with her.

It could be a big shock and we all agreed that a shock is the last thing she needs right now."

"What about the psychiatric hospital in Kalispell where Winona was supposedly sent? Did you check with them?"

He nodded. "I did look the hospital up."

"And?"

"It burned down forty years ago—and I doubt we would have gotten anywhere trying to question the people there, anyway. Patient confidentiality laws would've barred them from revealing anything to me or anyone else who came nosing around."

"Translation—you've essentially done nothing."

Now he seemed kind of sheepish. "Yeah. That's about the size of it."

She held out the old book again. "Please. I'm not staying in town. I'm taking a job in Bronco, starting a week from Monday."

"Doesn't matter," said Wilder. "Wren gave you the diary and I'm not taking it back."

* * *

Mel ended up bringing the old book home to the too-empty house she'd grown up in.

Todd Spurlock, her cheating ex-fiancé, texted her around ten. He'd been doing that, trying to get her to engage so he could beg her again to come back. She was fed up with that, so she blocked his number. That should do it for Todd.

And then, to distract herself from angry thoughts of the man who had messed up her life on too many levels, she picked up the old diary and started reading. It was pretty absorbing. She didn't stop until she read it through to its tragic end, using up half a box of Kleenex in the process.

The old book contained the sad story of Josiah Abernathy and his love affair with a woman he called "W." It was a story as old as time, really. The rich boy and the poor girl, the boy's disapproving parents. A forbidden love and an unplanned pregnancy—an "out of wedlock" pregnancy, as they used to say in whispers so long ago.

What became of the baby? In the diary, Josiah wrote that the child he and "W" named Beatrix had died at birth. And that "W" had suffered a breakdown at the loss. Josiah's parents had arranged for "W" to be cared for in a Kalispell psychiatric facility.

Late in the night, after she'd studied Josiah's journal cover to cover, Mel got out the envelope with her dear friend Winona's name on it and reread the letter that claimed baby Beatrix had lived.

By the time she finally went to sleep, it was nearing daybreak.

First thing Monday morning, Mel headed for the Rust Creek Falls Library and the archives of the *Rust Creek Falls Gazette*. She was looking for evidence that the Winona she knew and admired had been anywhere near Rust Creek Falls all those years ago.

Much to her surprise, she found a picture of a very young Winona waving a flag. Mel felt her throat clutching and a tear trailing down her cheek, just to see the pretty, vibrant woman Winona had once been. The photo was taken on Main Street during the annual Fourth of July Parade more than seventy years ago. The caption read "Miss Winona Cobbs waves the red, white and blue."

Mel visited Winona that afternoon. She found the old woman resting on the couch in her small living room. The network of wrinkles on her pale cheeks deepening with her welcoming smile, Winona sat up and reached for a hug. She let Mel brew them both some tea. They sipped and chatted about inconsequential things while Mel tried to find the right moment to bring up the story she'd read the night before.

She'd yet to find a way to broach the strange and difficult subject when Winona set her teacup and saucer aside. She had that look, the one she got when she knew something was bothering Mel.

For a moment, Mel felt eerily certain that her friend was about to announce that she, Winona, was the "W" of the journal, that she'd once loved Josiah Abernathy and ended up in the hospital when her baby was lost to her.

But then, very gently, Winona asked, "How's Todd?"

And Mel realized that Winona had picked up on the *other* thing that was bothering her. "You don't really want to hear."

"Yes, Mellie. I want to hear."

"Well, I don't want to go into detail about all that went wrong."

"That's all right, too. I just want you to know I'm here and ready to listen if you need to talk it over."

"Thank you. The downstroke is that Todd and I are over. I moved out of his house and I'm never going back to him."

"Where are you living?" Winona frowned. "Somehow, I don't see you moving back home to stay…"

Mel had lived in Bozeman for the past eight years, coming home in the summers and for holidays the first two years when her parents were still alive and less frequently after that. "No, I'm just in town for a few days. I've left Bozeman behind for good, though. In fact, I've got a temporary job waiting for me in Bronco. I start next week."

"Bronco," Winona echoed teasingly. "Aren't you the fancy one?"

In the heart of Montana, Bronco was a five-hour drive southeast from Rust Creek Falls. The town was well known as home to some of the wealthiest people in the state. "I'll be managing a new restaurant for DJ Traub."

"DJ Traub of DJ's Rib Shacks?"

"That's him."

"You worked in a Bozeman Rib Shack all through college, didn't you?"

"I did, yes. The Bronco DJ's is more upscale, though. It's called DJ's Deluxe and it's in Bronco Heights."

"Where all those rich people live."

"Yes, Winona," Mel said with a grin. "In the posh part of town."

"And you said the job in Bronco is temporary?"

"That's right. At the end of the year, I'm moving to Austin. I've already got something good lined up there. A company that tried to hire me more than once while I was in Bozeman is expanding into Texas. I'll be their finance and insurance manager. I have to tell you, I'm more than ready for a real change."

"You are such a go-getter." Winona gave her that strange little smile—the one that always had Mel thinking the old woman knew a lot more than she was saying. "But as for your move to Texas, we'll see, won't we?"

"It's happening, Winona. I'll be back now and then to visit you, and to look after the house." Though she had no plans to live in her hometown again, Mel had never been able to bring herself to sell her parents' house, so she rented it. Her last tenant had moved out a month ago—which meant it had been waiting for her when she'd left

Todd. The property manager she used had a new tenant moving in on August 1st. In the meantime, Mel had scheduled painters to freshen up a couple of the rooms and a handyman to take care of a couple of necessary repairs over the next few weeks.

"You won't move back to Rust Creek Falls and I understand that. I can see you're ready for something new. But Montana is your home," Winona insisted with a challenging gleam in her eyes. "I don't really believe Texas is where you're meant to be."

There was little point in arguing with Winona when she'd made up her mind. Mel settled for giving her friend a noncommittal smile. "As you said, we'll see..."

"You belong here in Big Sky Country, dear," Winona said gently. "You'll figure that out, I think." And then she seemed to sag a little. "Oh, I do get tired these days."

"Lie down, then. Get comfortable."

With a weary little sigh, Winona slipped off her shoes again and slowly stretched out. Mel got up and settled the afghan over her. As she leaned close, Winona reached out and brushed a hand, light as a moth's wing, against Mel's cheek. "You're a sweet girl, Mellie."

The diary, Mel thought. She still hadn't managed to bring it up to Winona—but really, where to even begin? So many questions had backed themselves up in her throat.

And Winona looked so frail. If the story Josiah Abernathy had written in the journal was true and Winona was his beloved "W," how would she respond to the startling news that the baby she'd believed had died so long ago might have lived, after all?

Wilder Crawford was probably right. Dumping something like that on a weakened woman in her nineties could cause a stroke or a heart attack.

And what good, really, would dredging up a tragic past do for Winona now?

Mel left Winona's little house without revealing what she knew.

First thing the next morning, she packed up her Audi Q7. The U-Haul she'd rented in Bozeman was already full of the few pieces of furniture and necessary household goods she'd taken from the house she'd shared with Todd. By 9:00 a.m., she was on her way to Bronco, where her interim job at DJ Traub's new restaurant was waiting, along with a studio apartment in a great building in Bronco Heights.

She took the old journal and its hidden letter with her—and no, she had no plans to pursue the mystery of Winona and Josiah and the lost baby Beatrix any further. But Wilder Crawford wouldn't take it back, so what else could she do?

Chapter One

Gabe Abernathy loved his family. But sometimes they made him a little bit crazy. Especially his dad. George Abernathy knew how a ranch should be run: *his* way. He didn't like anybody suggesting anything new or different—and "anybody" included his own 32-year-old son.

Mostly, Gabe let his dad run the ranch. He pitched in when needed and put his focus on his investments and property deals. Abernathy was an important name in Bronco and Gabe knew all the heavy hitters in the area. Luckily for his bank account, there were a lot of rich men—and women—in Gabe's hometown. And Gabe was on a first-name basis with most of them.

He still lived on the family ranch, though. He'd built his own place in a beautiful spot not far from the main house. Proximity to his parents had its benefits. It kept their family bond strong and he was there if they needed him. But living a few hundred yards from their front door also meant it was pretty much a given that now and then, he and his dad would lock horns. Gabe tried to pick his battles, but sometimes a man had to say what he thought.

Today had been one of those times. He and his dad had had words, an argument about overgrazing that went nowhere, as usual.

In the end, Gabe had tacked up Custard, his palomino gelding, and ridden out on the land to cool off.

The ride helped. The day was warm and breezy with a few cottony clouds floating around up there in the endless Montana sky, the kind of day that made a man count his blessings. Gabe was strong and smart and rich. His dad got on his last nerve now and then, but Gabe had nothing to complain about, really.

He clicked his tongue at Custard, stirring him to a canter and then to a gallop as they climbed the next rise. "Whoa, boy..." He drew the horse to a stop at the crest and leaned on the saddle horn.

Someone was trespassing.

Below, on the side of one of the winding dirt roads that crisscrossed the ranch, sat a silver SUV. It looked empty from Gabe's vantage point.

He clicked his tongue again and Custard took him down the other side of the hill to the vehicle.

He dismounted and circled the car, peering in the windows as he went. A yellow sweater was draped over the back of the passenger seat—a woman's sweater, soft-looking, with little pearl buttons. Through the passenger window, he spotted what looked like a zebra-patterned pouch in the side compartment of the driver's door. Makeup essentials, most likely.

Girlfriends on an adventure across private land? A definite possibility. They were probably harmless, but it never hurt to let tourists know that cattle could be dangerous and a working ranch was not a public park.

Right away, he found the footprints. There was only one set of them, after all. Leading Custard by the reins, his loaded rifle in his free hand, just in case, he followed the tracks of a pair of female-sized boots up over the next rise.

On the other side, the land sloped gently down to a copse of cottonwoods and the banks of Little Big Bear Creek, a narrow, swift-running stream that wound its way over a good portion of the Abernathy spread.

Maybe ten feet from the creek, a small blonde woman in jeans and a silky shirt the color of a ripe apricot sat on a blanket with a picnic basket at her side. She had her head in her hands. Her slim shoulders shook. Gabe could hear her sad little sobs.

As a rule, crying women made Gabe as uncomfortable as the next guy. He considered turning around and going back the way he'd come. But she looked so pitiful, her shoulders all hunched over in misery, her pretty wheat-colored hair falling in thick waves down her slender back. He had the strangest urge to comfort her at the same time as he felt he had no place intruding on a total stranger's private misery.

Then Custard let out a nervous snort.

The woman jumped up and whirled to face him, her streaming eyes widening at the sight of his rifle. Slowly, she put up her hands.

"Hey," he said gently, trying on a sheepish smile. "I'm not going to hurt you."

"You know what?" She dropped her hands with a forlorn little sigh. "Go ahead and shoot."

"Aw, now. You don't mean that..."

For a long moment, they simply regarded each other. Finally, she sniffed. "So you're *not* gonna shoot me?"

He engaged the safety and stuck the rifle back in the scabbard. "There. Just being cautious, that's all."

She tipped her head to the side as she regarded him. "Who *are* you?"

"I'm Gabe. I live here."

That brought a sad little laugh. "Just a lonesome cowboy, huh?"

"Pretty much." Yeah, okay. He was a long way from a poor cowpoke, but the woman was upset. The last thing she needed right now was some rich guy bragging about how much money he had. "Is it all right if I come down there?" When she gave him a slow nod, he led Custard on down to her, stopping a few yards from the blanket. "Mind if I join you?"

A tiny crease drew down between her sleek gold-kissed eyebrows. "Why?"

"You look like you could maybe use some company."

With a sniffle, she swiped tear tracks from her cheeks. "I came out here to be alone."

"Ah." The silence stretched out as they stared at each other. Even with her eyes and nose red from crying, she was gorgeous. He considered informing her that she was trespassing on private property. But really, it was obvious she only wanted to sit by the creek and cry in peace. "All right then, you be safe." He started back the way he'd come, Custard following placidly after him.

"Wait!" she called. When he paused and glanced back at her, she said, "On second thought, yeah."

"Yeah, I should join you?"

"Well, I mean, if you still want to."

"All right, then." He led his horse down to the creekside. It took only a minute to hitch Custard to a cottonwood. When he glanced at the woman again, she had dropped to the blanket. With a brave little smile, she patted the space next to her.

Not wanting to spook her any more than

he already had, he approached her slowly and took the spot she'd indicated, setting his hat on the blanket between them.

A little smile tugged on the corners of her soft mouth. Kind of devilish, that smile. She could get up to trouble, this one. And she had a look in those tear-damp blue eyes that said she wouldn't be putting up with any man's crap. He might have caught her in a weak moment, but if he thought he could get one over on her, he had another think coming.

He glanced up at the sky. "Pretty day."

She gave a little snort-laugh. "That the best you can do?"

He doubled down. "It's a *beautiful* day." And it was. That gentle breeze was still blowing, and the cottonwoods were kind of whispering together. The creek burbled in a cheerful way, glittering in the sun. A few clouds had gathered, creating dappled shadow on the ground as they drifted by overhead.

"I'm Melanie Driscoll. Call me Mel."

He looked at her again. It was a pure pleasure to do so. "Good to meet you, Mel."

"I'll bet you want to know why I've been bawling my eyes out, don't you?"

"I do want to hear, if you want to tell me."

That brought a small laugh and a long sigh. "I have to admit, there's something oddly safe about telling a stranger the things you don't have the heart to say to people you've known most of your life."

"I'm listening."

She blew out her cheeks with a hard breath. "It's nothing new or different. In fact, it's the oldest story in the book. A couple of weeks ago, I came home at lunch to find my fiancé, Todd, in bed with another woman."

"A cheater. Tell me you dumped his sorry ass."

"You bet I did. I threw his ostentatious diamond ring in his cheating face, packed a bag and left. He followed me out the door, swearing it was nothing, promising that it would never happen again."

"You didn't believe him." It wasn't a question.

"No, I did not. There *had* been others. I'd seen the signs, but I'd been kidding myself. Long story short, a few days later I went back to collect what few belongings I had. But I was definitely done with Todd. I quit my job with his family's company—because, yeah. Todd was the heir to the business where I'd been working my butt off since I graduated from Montana State. It was a job I loved, by the way. I'd made it to the top of the finance and insurance department." She pulled her knees up to her chest, rested her chin on them and stared off toward the creek. "Our plan, Cheating Todd's and mine, was to buy out his parents and run the place together. It was a tractor dealership. Spurlock's Farm Machinery."

Gabe knew of Spurlock's. A family business, a successful one, in Bozeman. "So then, you're from Bozeman?"

She shook her head. "Born and raised in Rust Creek Falls."

"Pretty country up there—and I'm sorry," he said. "At least about the job. Sounds like getting rid of Todd was a damn good move."

"Thank you, Gabe. I couldn't agree with you more." She stretched out her slim denim-clad legs, leaned back on her hands and spent several seconds regarding the thickening clouds overhead. "I went home to Rust Creek Falls for a few days. It's never been the same there for me, though. My folks were killed six years ago in a head-on collision with a long-haul trucker who fell asleep at the wheel."

"That's rough." He really did want to comfort her and had to remind himself not to reach out and touch her—maybe stroke her silky-looking hair or wrap an arm around her. He felt powerfully drawn to her, but he needed to remember that he didn't really know her and he had a responsibility to respect her space.

She shrugged, her face still tipped up to the sky. "Thus, the crying jag. And now,

I'm in Bronco till the first of the year, here to temporarily manage the new DJ's Deluxe restaurant in Bronco Heights—*and* put A-hole Todd firmly in my poor, broken heart's rearview mirror." Finally, she glanced his way.

He returned her wobbly smile with a relaxed one of his own. "What happens at the first of the year?"

"I'm moving to Austin, taking a job as F&I manager for a company similar to Spurlock's. Getting a whole new start in Texas, if you know what I mean."

Was it crazy that he was already thinking he didn't want her to go? "Maybe you'll discover how much you like it here, decide that Bronco is the right place for you."

"Not likely, Gabe. I'm ready for a major change."

"You'll miss Montana. The winters won't be long enough and the summers in Austin—way too hot and sticky."

They were looking at each other and they both kept on looking. It felt easy to him, not awkward or strange. It felt like they were sharing secrets with their eyes.

She broke the extended silence. "I have a picnic."

"I noticed the basket."

Those jewel-blue eyes glinted with humor. And invitation. "I'm willing to share."

"I would like that."

"All right, then." She pulled the basket closer and turned so she was sitting facing him. Moving the basket between them, she set out cheese and crackers, apple slices and grapes. She had a bottle of white wine and a corkscrew. "Do the honors?" she asked.

He opened the wine and poured it into the plastic Solo cups she'd brought.

They shared a toast to new beginnings. He was having a great time, his frustration with his father all but forgotten in the pleasure of just being with her. This was one of those great things that happen now and then in life—a magical encounter with a complete stranger.

She nibbled on a cracker and said what

he was thinking. "This is kind of magical, Gabe. I don't really even know you, but you've made me feel so much better about everything without really saying much of anything." She laughed, the sound soft and sweetly self-deprecating. "So far, I've done way more than my share of the talking."

"I like listening to you talk."

She sipped from her Solo cup, a thoughtful expression on her beautiful face. "We'll probably never see each other again…" She caught her lower lip between her pretty teeth. He longed to lean close and bite that lip for her.

As he considered his chances of stealing a kiss, a giant raindrop plopped on the basket. It was quickly followed by more.

They both glanced skyward—and with a flash of lightning and a hard crack of thunder, the heavens opened up in a downpour. They'd been so wrapped up in each other, neither of them had noticed that the clouds had grown thick and dark.

Mel let out an adorable shriek of surprised laughter as Custard gave a nervous whinny. "I'm soaked to the skin already!"

"Let's get out of here!"

She laughed again. "Good idea."

He helped her reload the basket, feeling a twinge of regret as she dumped the remaining wine out on the now-streaming ground.

He put on his wet hat. "I'll get the blanket." She stepped off it as he grabbed it up. "Come on. I'll take you to your car." Tossing the soaked wad of vinyl-backed flannel in front of the saddle horn, he untied Custard's reins. "Give me the basket."

"Wait—there's not enough room for both of us in that saddle."

"I know." The rain was a solid sheet of water pouring from the sky, loud enough he had to raise his voice to be heard over it. "I'll *walk* you to your car."

"It's not necess—"

"Yeah, it is." Gently, he took the basket from her and tied it to the saddle. "Okay then. Let's go."

She took his offered hand, her skin cool

and soft and dripping wet. They started up the rise, the rain a curtain all around them, Custard right behind them. It was a very wet walk, but at least it was quick.

At her Audi, she pressed her key fob to open the back hatch as he untied the basket. He handed it over and then gave her the muddy blanket. She tossed both inside and pressed the fob again to shut the hatch.

"Thank you, Gabe!" She stood there under the continued onslaught of the rain, gazing up at him through thick, wet eyelashes as water plastered her hair to her head and shoulders. It also streamed down her cheeks and over her chin and neck.

"Anytime," he said, not caring in the least if the two of them just stood there forever, practically drowning, having sex with their eyes.

"Can I give you a ride?" she asked.

"Nah. Me and Custard'll make it home just fine."

"You made a bad day so much better. Thank you."

"Yeah?" He couldn't stop looking at her mouth, so plump and inviting, shiny with the water pouring down over it.

"Oh, yeah—and I'd better get going…" She started to turn. He let Custard's reins drop and caught her arm before she could escape him. Those blue eyes got bigger. "What?"

"Give me your number."

A small sound of regret escaped her. "I am so tempted."

"Give in, then."

"Oh, Gabe…"

She really didn't need to say more. He got the message and reluctantly accepted it. Scooping off his streaming hat, he dropped it on the roof of the car. Now the rain poured directly on him again. He didn't care in the least. "If I can't have your number and I'm never going to see you again…"

Her gaze searched his face. "What?"

"I've been dying to do this." And he dipped his head to touch his wet lips to hers.

She sighed against his mouth, her breath warm, scented of apples and wine.

It was all the encouragement he needed. He dared to gather her to him, pulling her up to her tiptoes so he could feel her soft, slim body pressed nice and close.

But somehow, not close enough. He pulled her in even tighter and tasted her deeply.

It was magic, that kiss, everything he could have hoped for. A little crazy, kind of wild, beneath a streaming sky. He wanted it to last forever.

But it couldn't. When she pulled away a second time, he made himself let her go.

"Bye," she said, and turned away again. That time, he didn't try to stop her. A moment later, she had the driver's door open and was sliding in behind the wheel.

He grabbed his hat off the car's roof as she turned the engine over. And then he stood there, hat in hand, and watched her turn around and drive away. The Audi disappeared from sight and still he stood there, with the rain coming down in buckets, his eyes trained on the spot where she'd disappeared from his view, his arms feeling much too empty, his lips still tingling from the taste of that kiss—until Custard grew impatient. With a snort, the gelding butted him gently between the shoulder blades.

Gabe mounted up and turned Custard for home.

Mel drove toward Bronco in kind of a daze. Gabe the lonesome cowboy had kissed her!

And she'd let him. And it had been perfect. The kind of kiss that had a girl thinking maybe she didn't hate all men on principle, after all.

Very quickly, the rain slowed to a drizzle and then stopped altogether. The sun appeared and the clouds just melted away.

If she hadn't been soaking wet and sitting in a puddle behind the wheel, she might almost wonder if her picnic with Gabe and their kiss in the pouring rain had really happened.

It seemed like a dream to her. Magical. Unreal.

She felt almost breathless—because she was. She wished she'd just gone ahead and given him her number. Or at least that she'd gotten his last name.

But she hadn't. And really, wasn't that for the best? She was swearing off men indefinitely, focusing on *her* life and her own future. Even the hottest cowboy in Montana couldn't be allowed to distract her from her plans.

Still, her lips seemed to tingle all the way to the sprawling, upscale apartment complex in Bronco Heights where she would be living for the next six months or so.

It was called BH247, the complex. BH was for Bronco Heights, of course. And the 247? The street number on Serpentine Drive.

The complex pretty much had it all— indoor and outdoor pools, hot tubs, a big clubhouse and a fitness center. Her cute little studio even had a gorgeous view of the mountains.

She parked the Audi in her reserved space in the underground garage, gathered her soggy picnic stuff from where she'd tossed it in the back and took the elevator up to her floor.

On her own little service porch, she shoved the wet blanket into the high-efficiency apartment-sized front-loading washer. Next, she took off her mud-caked boots and then peeled off the rest of her clothes, adding the clothes to the load. Tossing in a detergent pod, she started the wash cycle.

Her boots she hauled back to the main room, where she dropped them in the sink. From there, she went straight to the bathroom for a long, lovely shower. After piling her acres of wet hair up into a haphazard knot, she pulled on shorts and a tank top and returned to the main room.

Twenty minutes later, she'd cleaned off her boots and unpacked what was left of the picnic. The boots and the drenched picnic basket she carried out to her small balcony to dry.

"Hey, neighbor," said a friendly female voice. It was coming from the balcony that adjoined hers.

Mel gave the picnic basket a nudge to tuck it under the eaves, where it would be safe from any future surprise downpours, and straightened. "Hi."

The gorgeous, pulled-together woman on the next-door balcony grinned at her. "I'm Brittany Brandt." She offered a smile.

They exchanged basic information. Mel explained that starting Monday, she would be managing the new DJ's Deluxe.

Brittany was unemployed. "Well, as of a couple of days ago," she said. "I'm an event planner. I was working for Evan Cruise— you know him?"

The name sounded vaguely familiar. "I think I saw his picture on a billboard on my way into town the other day. Dark-haired and intense-looking?"

"That's Evan."

"He does ghost tours, or something?"

"Yes, he does," said Brittany. "There are

lots of supposedly haunted places in Bronco Valley—abandoned mines, rusted oil rigs, tumbledown ranch houses with ghosts running around in them, that sort of thing. Evan does a big business with his tours. Unfortunately, he's a hard man to work for and he doesn't pay enough."

"So you quit?"

"Yes, I did. I've already got something new lined up, so I'm not complaining. Right now, I'm taking a short but much-needed break. And I was just about to drag my roomie away from her laptop and head out to the pool, get a little sun. Come with?"

Mel cast a wary glance up at the sky. "You think it'll rain again?"

Brittany laughed. "What's the worst that can happen? We'll already be wet."

"Good point." And it would be nice to get to know her new neighbors a little. "The outdoor pool, you said?"

"Yeah. Put on your suit. We'll meet you there."

* * *

By the time Mel joined her neighbors at the giant outdoor pool, the sky had cleared completely and the late-afternoon temperature was a balmy 80 degrees. Brittany and her roommate, Amanda Jenkins, had saved her one of the comfy cushioned poolside loungers.

Amanda was self-employed, a marketing manager who did most of her work on her laptop at home. She focused on social media campaigns and outreach for her clients. She and Brittany were both brunettes with brown eyes, but the similarity ended there. Tall, willowy Brittany had light-brown skin, an air of glamor and sophistication about her and an outgoing personality, while Amanda was petite, softly pretty and kind of quiet.

Mel liked them both. A lot. She found them fun and easy to talk to. For the second time that day, she said more than she probably should have about her cheating ex-fiancé and the great job she'd had to leave behind.

She even told them about her chance encounter with Gabe—because why not? They were good listeners and the good-looking cowboy was definitely on her mind.

"So there I am," she said, "with my pity-party picnic, out in the middle of who-knows-where, crying my eyes out over my lowlife, cheating ex and the great life I had to walk away from, when who should appear but a handsome cowboy, a rifle in one hand, leading a gorgeous palomino with the other."

Amanda seemed mildly alarmed. "Why the rifle? You don't look all that threatening to me."

"He was just being cautious, I think. He put the rifle away and asked if he could join me. I said yes."

"So this mysterious cowboy of yours wasn't the least shy, then." Brittany's low voice held more than a hint of irony.

"Not shy, but really sweet and understanding. And did I mention hot?" Mel pretended to fan herself. "And an amazing kisser, too."

Brittany gathered her glorious mane of natural curls in one hand and wrapped an elastic band around it, anchoring the thick mass into a high ponytail. "Has Gabe the Cowboy got a last name?"

"He didn't mention it." Both women looked puzzled. "Hey, it was just one of those things, you know? A great moment with a guy I'll never see again."

"But maybe we know him," argued Brittany. "Bronco's not as small as your hometown, but it's small-ish. And Amanda's got mad web skills. You give her Gabe-the-Cowboy's full name, she can find out way more than you ever wanted to know about him."

"But I don't need to know anything about him. That's the point. I'm not going to go looking for him. I've had enough of men to last me into the next decade, at least. But I had a great time with him and meeting him made me feel better about guys and life and everything, you know?"

"What did he look like?" asked Amanda.

"Does it matter, really?"

Brittany eased her designer sunglasses down her nose a fraction and gave Mel a long look over the top of them. "Humor us."

Mel threw up both hands. "Fine. Tall, lean, wide shoulders. Late twenties to early thirties. Light blue eyes, slightly spiky dark blond hair…"

"Well, that really narrows it down," Amanda said drily. "The good news is, the name Gabriel didn't become popular until the last twenty years or so."

Brittany was still looking at Mel over the top of her sunglasses. "Meaning there aren't a lot of Gabes who are the age you think *yours* is," she clarified.

"Gabe the Cowboy is in no way *mine*," Mel felt driven to insist. "And come on, Amanda, how can you even know that about his name?"

"Too much time online," said Brittany.

Amanda tapped the side of her head with a finger. "You'd be surprised the number of off-the-wall facts I've got stored in here."

"Ladies." Brittany clapped her hands sharply. "Can we please stay on task? Mel, we need more details. Close your eyes. Picture the guy..."

Why not? Mel played along. "Um, well, his silver belt buckle had a big *A* on it."

Brittany suggested, "Last-name initial, maybe?"

"Hold that thought." Amanda jumped up and headed for the building behind them.

When Mel shot a baffled glance at Brittany, she said, "Laptop."

"Ah."

A few minutes later, Amanda was back. She sat cross-legged on her lounger, her fingers flying over the laptop keys. "Hm," she said. "Yeah." She turned the laptop so that Mel and Brittany could see. "This shot appeared in the *Bronco Bulletin* last December—"

"That's him!" Mel cried. The picture

had been taken at some sort of white-tie event. Gabe wore a tux, of all things—and clearly not a rented one. He stood beneath a wrought-iron chandelier looped with Christmas garland and twinkly lights. A gorgeous redhead in evening dress clung to his arm.

"This was taken in the ballroom at the Association," said Amanda. "I know the venue because I did some outreach for them a few months ago and they gave me a tour of the buildings and grounds."

"It's a country club," said Brittany. "Or maybe you could call it a cattlemen's club. Seriously exclusive. Costs a fortune to join, but just having lots of money won't do it. To get in, you have to be sponsored by some-one who's already a member."

Amanda was nodding. "Your *poor* cow-boy, Gabe? He's from one of the richest families in town. The man has it all going on. Looks. Charm. Brains. Big money. And he's a heartbreaker, too. Lots of girls have tried to tame him, but he's never settled down."

"Of course, he hasn't," Mel muttered bitterly. At the same time, she couldn't help recalling how sweet and tender he'd been with her and—hold on just a minute.

What was the matter with her?

He was rich. Rich men were dangerous.

Plus, hadn't Amanda just said he was a player?

A player who'd lied to her, letting her think he was only a poor cowpuncher when in fact he had money to burn. The last thing she needed was another lying rich guy in her life.

Not that Gabe was in any way *in* her life. It was a chance meeting and they'd both agreed they would probably never see each other again.

Amanda went on, "The Abernathy spread is the second largest in the Bronco area."

Abernathy?

Mel popped bolt upright on the lounger.

"Wait. Abernathy, you said? Gabe's last name is *Abernathy*?"

"That's right." Amanda closed her laptop. "And Gabe's not only a rich rancher's son. He's branched out into property development. Made quite the success of it, too."

Brittany reached between their loungers and patted Mel's arm. "You okay?"

"Yeah, fine. It's just…" She thought of sweet, old Winona, who might or might not be the tragic young girl in Josiah Abernathy's diary. Could there actually be a connection between Gabe's family and the Rust Creek Falls Abernathys?

No.

Really. There were people named Abernathy all over the country and it was just a bizarre coincidence that Gabe was one.

Her new friends watched her with worried expressions. "What's the matter?" Amanda asked softly. "Are you okay?"

"Sorry." Mel played it off. "It's just, you know…men. Lying liars who lie."

"Oh, honey." Brittany shook her head with a sigh. "We hear you."

"And really," said Amanda, "maybe we shouldn't judge the guy."

"Please," Brittany scoffed at her friend. "You're too forgiving. You always have been."

But Amanda was insistent. "No, really. Look at it this way, Mel. Maybe Gabe *liked* that you thought he was just some ordinary cowboy—and yet you were interested in him, anyway."

By now, Mel just wanted to leave the subject of Gabe Abernathy behind. "I think I'll just stick with my first take on what happened with Gabe. He was kind to me when I was feeling low and I'm grateful for that."

At least she'd had sense enough not to give the guy her number. She'd been much too attracted to him and it would be way too easy to let him get under her skin.

Mel spent the next day purposely not thinking of Gabe Abernathy or any other guy. She puttered around her apartment and went out to dinner with Brittany and Amanda. Saturday was Independence Day. Mel attended the town parade and watched the fireworks from her balcony that night.

Sunday night, she climbed into bed early. She wanted to be fresh for her first day at DJ's Deluxe. It would be a long shift tomorrow. She would go in around noon and meet the current manager, who would introduce her to the rest of the staff and bring her up to speed. Dinner service was the main event, so of course she would be there for that.

Sleep was elusive, though. After a couple of hours of punching her pillow and tossing around, she ended up turning the light back on, propping her pillows against the headboard and pulling open the nightstand drawer, where she'd stuck the diary that Wilder Crawford had refused to take back.

In the lamplight, the gemstones on the front glittered at her as if in welcome. She reminded herself that she'd already read the sad story cover to cover. She needed to shut the drawer and turn off the light.

But she didn't. She got out the diary and read it again. It was just as sad the second time. She cried at the end. And then she blew her nose and dried her eyes and read the brief letter addressed to a girl named Winona who had the same last name as the kind old woman who lived up the street from her parents' house in Rust Creek Falls.

She fell asleep like that, with the lamp still on, the diary open across her knees and the creased letter in her hands.

In the morning, her neck ached from sleeping sitting up and she had to go heavy on the concealer to cover the dark circles beneath her eyes.

DJ's Deluxe had a whole different feel than the DJ's Rib Shacks that had made DJ Traub famous. Instead of picnic-table ambiance, the interior was all rich woods with accents of hammered copper and brushed nickel. The long bar was a shiny expanse of gleaming teak. Somehow, the restaurant managed to be warm, inviting—and exclusive. The place had a casual feel, but in a very upscale way.

Mel spent the day shadowing the current manager, who left at six.

Gwen Fox, the assistant manager, took over. Mel followed Gwen around the front of the house until seven, greeting customers, making sure everyone was happy with the food and the service. It was your usual Monday night in the restaurant business, meaning the pace was slower than most nights, a good night to train.

At seven, she left Gwen to handle the front of the house and went into the kitchen where the chef, Damien Brutale, ruled. Her plan was to help expedite if necessary, but really, she just wanted to observe, watch the staff get the food out, see how efficiently they worked together, get a feel for everything they were doing right as well as for what might need improvement in the future.

She'd been in the kitchen for five minutes, max, when Gwen came racing down the hallway from the dining room. "Mel." Mel left the serving line and went to her. "A customer would like to speak with you."

"They asked for the manager?" Since Mel was training for the next few nights, Gwen would logically have dealt with any customer issues.

"No. He asked for you by name."

"Has this customer got a name?"

Gwen leaned a little closer. "It's Gabe Abernathy."

Chapter Two

"I know you're new to Bronco," Gwen said, keeping her voice low. Confidential. "Do you know Gabe?"

Annoying butterflies danced a ridiculous jig in her belly, but Mel kept her voice noncommittal. "We met the other day. Briefly."

"You don't know him well, then?"

"No. Not at all, really." Okay, yeah. She *had* laid practically her whole life story on him and then kissed him with some serious tongue. But still, that didn't mean she *knew* the guy.

"Heads up, then. The Abernathys are an important family around here."

She knew that already, courtesy of Amanda and Brittany. And why had she made the mistake of telling him her full name and where she would be working? "Thanks, Gwen."

"He's at the bar."

"I'll just go and see what he wants, then…"

Mel found him sitting alone at one end of the bar. Looking all kinds of gorgeous in dark-wash jeans, a crisp white shirt and a lightweight jacket, he already had a whiskey, neat, in front of him.

As soon as he spotted her, his fine mouth quirked with a grin. He patted the empty stool next to him.

She moved close but didn't take the offered seat. "Gabe." She leaned an elbow on the bar. "Got a problem with the service?"

"The service is excellent."

"How was your meal?"

"Right now, I'm just enjoying a drink— and admiring the view." His gaze skated over her black pencil skirt and white silk shirt. "Very professional."

"Thank you. So then, no complaints on the service and you haven't ordered yet. What can I do for you?"

Those clear blue eyes made a bunch of intimate suggestions. "How's the new job going?"

"Surprisingly smoothly for a first day."

"Glad to hear it."

"Gabe, why are you here?"

"I like this place. I eat here often."

"Well, all right. Tonight, I'm training. Gwen is the one you should ask for if there's anything special you need."

He seemed to be studying her. The silence between them spun out. Finally, he asked, "When's your first night off?"

She considered refusing to tell him. But he would only keep after her until she gave it up. "Thursday." She knew what was coming next.

And she was right. "Let me take you out to dinner Thursday night."

"It's not a good idea."

"Why not?"

She glanced at the bartender, who seemed to be minding his own business setting up drink orders for one of the waitresses and taking care of the customers at the other end of the bar. "Are you pursuing me, Gabe?"

He gave her that killer grin again. "Damn straight."

"Well, pursuing me will get you nowhere. Remember that cheating fiancé I mentioned the other day?"

"How could I forget?"

"He chased me. I knew it wasn't smart to get involved with the boss's son. I kept saying no. He kept asking. Took him a year to get a date. My mistake. I never should have said yes to him. Todd Spurlock was a lesson I won't forget."

"I'm not Cheating Todd, Mel. I think you know that."

She held his gaze and kept her voice low and firm. "I mean it, Gabe. It's not going to happen."

"I like you. I want to see you again."

She wrapped her arms around her middle to keep from gesturing wildly with them. "Have you heard a word I've said?"

"Yep. You have my undivided attention." The quietly spoken statement caused more of those fluttering sensations in her belly.

"What I'm trying to make you understand is that this time, I'm not letting myself be caught. Chasing me will get you nowhere."

He picked up his drink and took a sip, setting the glass back down with care. "How many ways can I say it? I'm not Todd."

"But you did lie to me. You pretended to be a broke cowboy."

"No, I didn't. You asked who I was. I gave you my name."

"Just your *first* name," she accused.

"If you'd asked, I would have told you my last name, too. But you didn't. I said that I lived there—and I do. Did you know you were on Abernathy land?"

She'd had no clue. "No, I did not."

"Well, there you go. Then you called me

a lonesome cowboy and I said that I was. I can rope and ride and I've been working around cattle since I learned how to walk. The way I see it, that makes me a cowboy. As for the lonesome part, sometimes I do feel kind of lonely, so I qualify on that score, too."

She scoffed. "You're a rich guy from an important local family."

He picked up his glass again and kind of wiggled it at her. "You sure you don't want a drink?"

"No, thanks."

"So about Thursday night? I'll pick you up at seven."

Did the man ever give up? "You're not getting it. There's also a big problem with your name."

"What? Now you don't like the name Gabe for some reason? My full name is Gabriel. You can call me that."

"I like Gabe just fine. It's your *last* name I'm not comfortable with."

"Okay, I'll bite. What's wrong with Abernathy?"

"There were Abernathys in Rust Creek Falls."

"There are Abernathys a lot of places."

"Well, in Rust Creek Falls, so the story goes, the Abernathys sold off their ranch and left town suddenly, without a trace. Like in the dead of night, never to be seen or heard from again. At the time, there was a lot of whispered speculation about the things those Abernathys got up to, the kinds of things that would make a whole family run away in the night. They were a shady bunch, the Abernathys of Rust Creek Falls."

He gave a low laugh. The sound made the nerve endings tingle up and down her spine. "That's quite a story, Mel."

"It's a known fact that you can't trust an Abernathy."

"You're just yanking my chain," he accused in a low, sexy rumble.

She had to press her lips together to keep from smirking. "You can take it."

"Have lunch with me tomorrow out at the ranch. I'll introduce you to Malone. He's been the family cook for longer than I can remember. You'll love him. You can ask him anything you want about me and he'll give it to you straight. Malone knows where all the bodies are buried."

"There are bodies?" Should she be alarmed?

"Settle down, Mel. It's just a figure of speech."

"I'm serious," she insisted. "I'm not falling for any of your lines."

"Lunch." He kept pushing. "Just lunch…"

Actually, she *was* kind of curious to see his ranch. And maybe this Malone person had Abernathy family secrets he would share. Maybe the Bronco Abernathys had some connection to the ones who had vanished from Rust Creek Falls. Maybe the answers to the questions posed by Josiah's diary had been right here in Bronco all this time, just waiting for her to come and root them out.

Yeah. Hardly likely.

However, having all the dirt on Gabe could be fun. She really wasn't going to date the guy. But her so-called lonesome cowboy was wildly attractive and she very much enjoyed giving him a bad time. Lunch at his ranch could present any number of delicious opportunities to rattle his cage.

Then again, being near him was kind of like wandering into Daisy's Donuts back home and ordering a dozen of their amazing maple bars—all the while promising herself she would only eat one. The man was too tempting by half and the whole idea was *not* to fall for another smooth-talking rich guy.

No, she reminded herself. *Just tell him no.* But when she opened her mouth, what came out was, "Lunch. Tomorrow. At your ranch. But it's not in any way a date. I'm just, you know, curious about what the Bronco Abernathys are really like."

That got her his full-on smile. It was nothing short of a secret weapon, that smile. All of a sudden, her cheeks felt hot. Was she blushing? The gleam in his eyes said she was. "Give me your number and your address," he instructed. "I'll pick you up at—"

"Uh-uh. I'll drive myself."

"I'll still need your number to text you directions."

She should grab a napkin and tell him to write the directions down. But maybe that would be skirting a little too close to out-and-out bitch mode. "Give me your phone," she said.

He picked it up off the bar, unlocked it and passed it over. She sent herself a text. Her phone buzzed in her pocket.

"Be there at eleven," he said. "I'll show you my place and then we can walk over to the main house to eat. It'll be casual, buffet-style. But Malone always puts out a good spread. I'll arrange for you to talk to Malone privately, so you can find out all my dirty secrets. You can also meet my dad and mom—don't freak." Had he seen the panic in her eyes? "I get it. You're not in the market for a boyfriend and you don't want to meet *any* guy's parents. But they live there and lunch in the main house is kind of a thing. You can ask them questions, make up your own mind about the Bronco Abernathys. You're going to find we're not as shifty as you seem to think."

The next day, Mel had no trouble finding her way to the Abernathy ranch.

It took maybe twenty minutes to reach the turnoff from the state road. A few minutes later, she was driving right past the spot where she'd parked for her impromptu picnic the other day.

The ranch was beautiful—rolling, open land where cattle grazed peacefully under the endless sky. Fields of wildflowers stretched off toward the mountains, small stands of cottonwoods and the occasional tall pine dotting the landscape here and there.

It was almost eleven when she made the final turn down the long, graveled driveway that led to a cluster of buildings in the distance. Up ahead, one of those fancy iron ranch signs arched over the road, with rustic split-rail fencing running off into the distance on either side. On the rolling prairie land beyond the sign, she could make out giant barns, several sheds and a few large houses scattered about on low, rolling hills.

Gabe and his family had clearly done all right for themselves.

Her pleasure at the sheer beauty of the setting vanished completely, though, when she got close enough to read the sign.

In black wrought iron, stretching over the road with a wagon wheel mounted to either side, was the name of the ranch.

The Ambling A.

The sight had her hitting the brakes hard enough that she bumped her head on the rearview mirror.

"Ouch!" For a minute, she just sat there with her foot on the brake, the car idling in the middle of the graveled road, rubbing her head, more than a little creeped out.

How likely was it that a random family named Abernathy in Bronco would call their ranch by the same name as the Abernathys who had suddenly vanished from Rust Creek Falls?

Didn't it make more sense that the Abernathys from her hometown were related somehow to Gabe's family, that they'd named their ranch here after the one in Rust Creek Falls—or possibly the other way around?

She would have to look into it. Maybe. As soon as the hair on the back of her neck stopped standing on end every time she thought about it.

Maybe Gabe's family had heard of the other Ambling A and decided they liked the name. But if they had, wouldn't Gabe have said something last evening when she'd given him a hard time about those other Abernathys running away in the dead of night?

And wait. Was she making a really big deal out of nothing at all?

Probably.

Easing her foot off the brake, she drove on, under the sign, past an ostentatious log-cabin mansion to a slightly smaller place of natural stone and cedar, with log accents and lots of big windows.

Gabe greeted her at the wide, rough-hewn front door wearing faded jeans, rawhide boots and a worn plaid shirt with the sleeves rolled to the elbows. He looked more like the lonesome cowboy she'd met that first day than the rich man who'd shown up at DJ's last night.

For a long, sweet minute or two, he just stood there in the doorway, grinning like the sight of her had made his day. "Right on time."

There ought to be a law against men as good-looking as Gabe. "I had excellent in-structions. And Google Maps."

He stepped back and ushered her inside, where a lean, brown-spotted dog sat look-

ing up at her hopefully through big choco-
late-brown eyes.

"Who's this?" she asked.

"Butch."

"German shorthair?"

"Most likely. And Lab and maybe beagle.
Butch is a little bit of everything. Go ahead
and say hi."

The mutt let out a whine of happiness as
she knelt to stroke his head and give him a
good scratch down his back.

"He's one of Daphne Taylor's rescues,"
Gabe explained. "Daphne's a rebel, I guess
you might say. The Taylors are arguably
the most influential family in town. They
have a hand in just about everything that
goes on around here, but Daphne's kind of
turned her back on all that. She runs an animal sanctuary called Happy Hearts. You
want a dog or cat or maybe a goat, a chatty
parrot or a really good-natured pig, I'll introduce you to Daphne."

A pet? She hadn't had a pet since her senior year in high school when her child-

hood cat, Bluebonnet, headed off to that big scratching post in the sky. Todd, the cheating jerk, had been allergic to pet dander—or so he'd always claimed. "I'm not sure they even allow pets in my building. But an animal sanctuary, that sounds interesting."

"Say the word. I'll take you there." He was giving her that look again, the one that melted her midsection and lowered her IQ by several points.

"Not going out with you," she reminded him, her voice strangely husky to her own ears.

"It's not a date if we go to Daphne's animal sanctuary. It's me helping you to put an end to your sad state of petlessness."

The man was just way too good at this. He elevated flirting to a high art. "I'll think it over."

"Can't ask for more," he said mildly.

"Right." He could and he would and they both knew it, too. "Your house is beautiful."

"I had it built a couple of years ago. The main house has plenty of room, but my dad and I get into it now and then. It's better having my own place to go to. Come on. I'll give you a quick tour."

He led her through the rooms. The living area had floor-to-ceiling windows, vaulted wooden ceilings and a huge natural stone fireplace with a mantel made of a giant log. In the rustic-style kitchen, she admired the gorgeous granite counters and chef-quality appliances. As for the master suite, you could fit her whole apartment inside it with room to spare. The bath in there had heated slate floors, dual vanity sinks, a walk-in shower and a big clawfoot tub.

"You live here alone?" she asked as he led her back to the living room.

"Just me and Butch. But I'm open to sleepovers."

"I'll bet you are."

He took a step closer. "I'll even let you soak in my clawfoot tub." His quiet, slightly rough voice stirred her, made her think of long, wet kisses shared in a big, comfy bed.

She could smell his aftershave, clean and

woodsy, and his mouth looked so soft, in perfect counterpoint to his sculpted jaw and hard, lean body. It would be so easy to sway toward him. His sky blue eyes promised that if she kissed him again, she wouldn't regret it.

No. Uh-uh. Not happening. "Nope. No sleepovers."

He looked at her so tenderly. Patiently, too. As though he could wait forever for her to say yes. "The offer's open if you change your mind."

At lunch, she met Gabe's mother and father, George and Angela, and his grandfather, Alexander. Alexander, she learned, had three brothers. Each of those brothers had children and grandchildren. There was even a great-grandchild or two. Gabe not only had a large extended family in the area, he also had a sister, Erica, who lived in Denver and rarely visited her family in Bronco.

After they loaded up their plates at the

buffet, they sat clustered together at one end of the long dining room table under an antler chandelier and facing a big window with a spectacular view of tall peaks in the distance. Mel considered casually mentioning that there was an Ambling A Ranch in Rust Creek Falls, too, and that a family named Abernathy had once owned it.

But she knew that if she started in about the Rust Creek Falls Abernathys, she wouldn't sound casual at all. She might end up blurting out everything—telling these people she'd just met about her friend Winona who might or might not have loved a man named Josiah Abernathy, had his child and ended up in psychiatric care when the baby died—except, maybe the baby hadn't died, after all...

No. It just wasn't a conversation to be having over lunch with people she'd never met before. Mel needed time.

She needed to mull over this eerie turn of events, to deal with the uncomfortable sense she was getting that Wilder Crawford might have been right—not about her finding true love. That was not happening. But about the mystery of the missing baby Beatrix.

Had fate somehow handed her the diary and then guided her to the place where the mystery might be solved?

It seemed way beyond far-fetched. But still, it had also started to feel eerily possible, somehow.

Not long after they sat down, Gabe and his dad got into a minor dispute over bison, of all things. Gabe was pushing to introduce a small herd to the ranch.

Bison meat was becoming more and more popular in stores and restaurants, Gabe argued, and raising bison beat out cattle in terms of the cost and sustainability. Bison could live on wild grasses and didn't require special shelter in the cold months. Plus, they didn't congregate by ponds and creeks like cattle did, flattening the grasses and sometimes contaminating their water sources.

"We're a cattle operation," George said sternly.

"Always have been, always will be." Alexander bobbed his white head in agreement with his son. "No self-respecting rancher raises bison, my boy. A bison is a wild animal."

"Exactly," Gabe agreed. "And a wild animal does a lot better job of taking care of itself and the land that it grazes on."

"Mel." In a clear bid for a change of subject, Gabe's mom cut in. "Tell us a little about yourself. Where are you from? What brings you to Bronco?"

Mel explained briefly about her upbringing in Rust Creek Falls and the loss of her parents. She said she'd lived in Bozeman for several years. From there, leaving out her job at Spurlock's and the disaster that was her engagement to Todd, she skipped right on to how she'd come to Bronco to work at DJ's Deluxe.

Gabe's mom had more questions, about her education and her life in Bozeman.

Gabe cut in. "Mom. Enough. You'll scare her away."

Angela laughed and let it go.

"I like your folks," Mel said later, when they'd finished lunch and Gabe had led her out to sit in the log chairs on the long front porch, just the two of them, with Butch snoozing nearby.

"My dad's kind of stuck in his ways and my mom gives the FBI a run for its money when she starts in with one of her interrogations."

"Just like parents everywhere."

"True."

"And you're lucky you still have them," she reminded him softly.

"You're right." He gazed at her in a warm, steady way that almost made her want to forget she'd sworn off men. When he looked at her like that, she was seriously tempted to announce that she'd love to go out with him, and yes, a sleepover in his bed and a long soak in his clawfoot tub sounded like the best plan ever. Especially if he would be climbing in the tub with her.

The front door opened and a tall, craggy-faced cowboy who looked a little younger than Gabe's grandfather came out. He had a mustache and graying hair.

Gabe stood. "Malone. There you are. I want you to meet Mel."

Not sure whether to feel relieved or disappointed at the interruption, Mel got up, too. She shook the old man's leathery hand. "Lunch was delicious."

"I'm glad you enjoyed it."

Gabe said, "I'll leave you two alone for a while."

She grabbed his arm, which was solid and strong, just like the rest of him. "Wait." He glanced down at her hand on him and then up into her eyes. She felt her cheeks coloring as she let go. "You sure? I can ask anything?"

His mouth hitched up in a smile that curled her toes inside her ankle boots.

"Anything." He nodded at Malone. "Tell her the truth about me."

"You know I will," said the old man.

And Gabe went inside, leaving Mel standing there trying to decide what questions to ask. She dropped back into the giant log chair. "Have a seat."

"Don't mind if I do." Malone lowered himself into the chair Gabe had vacated. "Ask away."

"You're, um, the expert on Gabe, then?"

"Well, now, I *have* been with this family for more than twenty years. I've seen all the Abernathys in action, you might say. And I've known Gabe since he was a knobby-kneed youngster."

She couldn't resist teasing the old guy a little. "But can I trust you to tell me the truth about him?"

"I make it a point to shoot straight. Ask any man who knows me."

"Well, all right, then. Is Gabe a liar?"

"He is not."

She shook a finger at him. "When I met him, he pretended to be a poor cowboy."

Malone sat up straighter. "He told you right out that he was broke?"

"Well, no. But when I called him a lonesome cowboy, he didn't say he wasn't."

"Young lady, I do not see how you can call that a lie. Gabriel Abernathy has been ropin' and ridin' since he was knee-high to a gnat. If that doesn't qualify him as a cowboy, I don't know what does. And as for the 'lonesome' part—"

"Okay, okay." She patted the air between them with both hands. "That's pretty much what he said when I jumped all over him about it."

"Then why are you askin' me?"

"It never hurts to cross-check a man's story."

Malone gave her a long, squinty-eyed stare. "I don't mean to offend, Mel, but you got trust issues, I think."

Why deny it? "Oh, yes, I do."

"Well, I stick by my previous statement. Gabriel Abernathy is no liar."

"Has he ever cheated—on a test, over money, on a woman he was seeing?"

"'Course not."

Actually, this was kind of fun. "Is Gabe an ass?"

Malone gave a low snort of laughter. "No, but he's pretty damn sure of himself. All the ladies seem to love him."

"So I've heard," she muttered.

"He's yet to find the girl for him, so I see no problem there. A man has a right to keep searching till he finds what he's looking for."

"Some men do find what they're looking for—but they keep on searching, anyway. Just for the fun of it, I guess."

"You mean they cheat."

"That's right."

"I'll say it again. Gabe is no cheater. As long as he hasn't promised his heart, he has every right to step out with any pretty lady he likes—that is, given that the lady in question is willing and unattached."

"Has Gabe ever been in love?"

"I do not believe so."

Her phone buzzed in her pocket. "Excuse me." She took it out and saw she had a text from a number she didn't recognize.

You blocked me. Why?

Todd. Suddenly, her stomach felt twisted and she wanted to break her own phone. She thumb-typed a swift response. Leave me alone. I will block you again.

How can you be so unforgiving? I love you. You're the only woman for me.

You mean aside from that woman I found in our bed with you? Never mind. Don't answer that. Goodbye, Todd.

She blocked that number, too, and put the phone away.

When she glanced up, the old guy was

watching her. "I'm sorry, Malone. Where were we?"

"You look mad as a peeled rattler. What was that all about?"

She almost played the question off, but that would be lying and she'd just made a big deal about her contempt for liars. "It's my ex-fiancé. He cheated on me and I left him and now he won't stop trying to convince me he deserves another chance."

The old guy reached out and gently patted her hand. His kind touch had her eyes misting over. "Once a man cheats," Malone said, "it gets really hard to trust him again."

"I will *never* trust him again."

"And, though I've always believed in second chances, I can't help thinking you're wise. Stay strong, Mel." Gently, he added, "But don't be afraid to give a better man a chance."

She drew a slow, slightly ragged breath. "Where were we?"

Malone launched into a cute story about the first horse Gabe had trained himself.

"That pesky horse kept throwing him, and Gabe just climbed right back on—and got thrown again. The horse gave up first. In the end, that horse was a marvel. Bred as a cutting horse. Gabe trained him right and he lived up to his potential, had that uncanny ability to read each and every move of any given cow. Pure poetry, watching that horse work."

Mel asked, "Was Gabe a troublesome kid?"

"He was curious. Determined. He got into scrapes and then managed to find a way to get out of them, mostly without major consequences. He was honest. Even as a child, anyone could see he had a good heart. You could do worse, Mel."

"Too bad I'm not looking for a man," she replied and hit him with more questions. Malone answered each one thoughtfully, with a touch of charming humor.

When Gabe, with Butch at his heels, emerged from the house, Malone got up.

"I did my best. She's a tough customer, this one."

"That was fun," she said, once Malone had gone back inside.

"So?" Gabe spread his arms wide. "What's the verdict? Hit me with it."

"I'll say this much. You don't suck."

He let out a low laugh. "Is that all I get?"

"Hey. Malone works for you. How can I be sure he's going to tell me the worst about you?"

"Give a guy a break, Mel."

"I like you, okay?" She *more* than liked him. But it didn't matter. She refused to get anything started with him. "It's just not going to happen."

"But you *do* like me."

"Didn't I just say I did?"

He dropped into the chair at her side again. "The way I see it, I'm bound to get through eventually."

"I'm a bad bet."

"Don't say that. It's not true."

"Yes, it is. I'm still bitter about my rotten ex—and anyway, I'm leaving in a few months, remember? You should probably just give up on me now."

Undeterred, he shot her that gorgeous grin of his. "Aw, Mel. I'm no quitter. Malone should have mentioned that. And from now until January is a very long time."

Chapter Three

That night at DJ's, the bar was packed until after seven. Mel stepped in to help the bartender with setups and to serve beer and a few of the simpler drinks.

When things slowed down a little, she went back out on the floor. She'd just made the rounds of all the tables and dropped in at the hostess station to make sure all was well there when she glanced over at the now-quiet bar and saw Gabe sitting on the same stool as last night, watching her. When their gazes met, he gave her his slowest, sexiest smile, the one that almost had her seeing rainbows and unicorns.

Ridiculous. Truly. You'd think she would have learned her lesson by now. Rainbows never lasted. They appeared in that too-brief moment after a storm—and then vanished as though they'd never been. As for unicorns, they didn't exist in the first place.

As soon as she had a spare minute, she went over there, sliding into the space between his stool and the next one, just like the night before. "Two nights in a row." She wore her most professional, impersonal smile. "You must really like it here."

"I do." His sky-blue gaze swept over her. "The food is excellent, the atmosphere manages to hit the perfect middle ground between comfortable and exclusive. And the bartender knows my drink." He toasted her with his glass of whiskey.

"Just here for a drink, then?"

"I'm meeting some business associates for dinner."

"Ah." A business dinner. Nothing to do

with her. Good. He'd gotten the message. She should be relieved. And she was—relieved, not disappointed. Not disappointed in the least. "Well, have a productive meeting, then."

"Mel." His warm fingers brushed her forearm as she started to turn. Heat bloomed at the light touch and flowed upward, to her shoulder, over her neck. Her cheeks felt hot.

Oh, this was bad.

Chemistry. Why did it have to be so hard to ignore?

She blasted him another plastic smile. "Yes?"

He leaned her way just a little. "Have dinner with me. Thursday night."

So then. He might have a dinner meeting, but he was here to see her, too. A little thrill shot through her. She just knew her blush was deeper than ever.

Really, what was the matter with her? She was becoming one of those women, the kind who said they wanted one thing—while wishing way too hard for another.

"I'm not going to do that. You have to stop asking me."

"Sorry. But I'm not ready to give up on you yet, Mel. I'm just not. See, I have this really strong feeling that giving up on you would be a big mistake."

She scoffed, but the sound was weak. "Oh, come on. You make it sound like life and death. It's only a date."

"Exactly." He gave her that smile that somehow annihilated her will to resist him. "Only a date. Not a big deal. You just need to say yes."

"No. Really—and I have to go now. I'm working."

"I'm not giving up."

"Enjoy your dinner, Gabe." That time, when she turned away, he let her go.

The rest of his party arrived a few minutes later. Mel was much too aware of where the hostess seated them, of the occasional sound of his low laughter in response to something one of the others at the table had said. The dinner meeting went on for a couple of hours. Mel switched places with Gwen at nine thirty and the next time she emerged from the kitchen, he was gone.

But he came back on Wednesday. She turned around at a little before seven and there he was, in the spot she'd already come to think of as his, at the end of the bar.

She really tried not to go over there. But she didn't try hard enough.

Ten minutes after she first spotted him, she slipped into the space between his stool and the next one over. "Another business dinner?"

"Nope. Tonight I'm just here to see you. Tomorrow's your night off. Spend it with me."

Yes. The word kind of bounced around in her brain and almost leapt out her mouth. But she kept her lips pressed together and shook her head slowly.

He studied her for a long, intense minute or two. "You off all day tomorrow?"

Still half-afraid to say anything for fear she'd find herself agreeing to go out with him, she nodded. And then he was grinning. And then suddenly, they were both laughing. Because she refused to answer his question and he seemed to have a pretty good idea why.

Then he asked, "How about a visit to Daphne Taylor's animal sanctuary? We'll go in the afternoon. It won't in any way be a date. You might find a pet. Or you might just enjoy having a look around."

She really was curious about that animal sanctuary…

"Come on," he coaxed. "You know you're curious about Happy Hearts."

Now he read minds? "How can you possibly know that?"

He was definitely smirking. "It'll be fun. And you'll love Daphne."

She made the mistake of opening her mouth yet again. A yes popped out. "All right. What time?"

"I'll pick you up at noon."

"You don't have my address."

"Text it to me."

This was the moment to insist she would take her own car.

But really, if she was meeting him there anyway, why not just ride with him? She pulled out her phone and sent the text.

His phone, right there on the bar by his elbow, lit up. He shot her a grin. "Great." And then he pulled some bills from his pocket, dropped them on the bar next to his glass and grabbed the phone. "See you at noon."

"I don't need a pet," she warned, though it just so happened that yesterday as she was leaving for work, she'd seen a calico cat basking in some unknown neighbor's window at BH247. The cat had her thinking of her sweet, lost Bluebonnet again, feeling a little wistful, maybe. It wouldn't be such a bad thing to have a furry friend to keep her company. This morning, she'd checked her lease. Her building allowed cats and small dogs, though the lease required that pet owners pay a rather hefty deposit for possible damages—not that it even mattered. She was *not* getting a pet.

Gabe wore a serious expression, but humor danced in those beautiful eyes of his. "No pets for you. Got it."

"And this isn't a date," she reminded him.

"Not a date, no way," he agreed.

"Just so we understand each other."

"We do, Mel. We understand each other perfectly." With a last nod, he turned and headed for the exit.

Daphne Taylor came right out to greet them when Mel and Gabe arrived at Happy Hearts Animal Sanctuary.

The daughter of the richest man in Bronco, Daphne was slim and serious, her pretty face free of makeup. She hugged Gabe, greeted Mel warmly and then gave them a tour of the farm where she made a home for a wide variety of animals in need.

Mel loved the place. She petted the horses and laughed at the antics of the baby goats.

After Daphne left them to their own devices, Gabe led Mel to a big barn not far from where he'd parked his giant four-door pickup.

"This barn is just for the cats and dogs," he explained as he led her through the entry door.

The big, wood-sided structure had cat quarters on one side and a place for the dogs on the other, each area with its own separate outdoor enclosure attached. Daphne had helpers, mostly volunteers, who cared for the animals and supervised the dogs whenever they were taken out to play.

The cats' yard was screened on the sides and above. It had comfy spots for basking in the sun and a series of cat runs going every which way.

And there were kittens. Lots of kittens. They had their own room in the barn. Until the kittens were weaned, their mamas lived there with them. The kitten room was filled with randomly stacked hay bales for the little ones to climb and play on.

Mel and Gabe stood at the glass wall that

kept the kittens contained and watched the action on the other side. "There are so many," she said.

"Yeah. A lot of people abandon pregnant cats. Anyone who adopts a Happy Hearts cat pays a discounted amount upfront for spaying or neutering."

"Good."

Beyond the glass wall, kittens jumped around on the hay bales, playing with each other, getting in little tussles, rolling off the bales and then leaping right up and climbing them again.

"You want to go in?" Gabe asked. He was standing very close, close enough that she could see the darker rims around his pale blue irises and breathe in his woods and citrus scent.

"It's okay?"

A teenager in a Happy Hearts T-shirt lugging a giant bag of kibble paused on his way to the adult cats' feeding area. "Just be sure to keep the door closed and the kittens inside."

"Come on," said Gabe. "You know you want to." His expression seemed to hint at more than just petting kittens.

They went in and a few of the kittens came prancing right over to them. "They're all so adorable." She scooped up a long-haired gray one with fluffy white paws. It was already purring. "Aww. Little sweet-heart…" Perching on a hay bale, she held the kitten close and buried her nose in its thick, hay-scented fur. "My cat, Bluebonnet, was gray, with big blue eyes."

The kitten glanced up at her. This one had luminous amber eyes. Gabe dropped down on the hay bale with her, close enough that she could feel the warmth of him. His thigh brushed hers, denim on denim, sending a heated little shiver racing over her skin. "It's a cutie, that one."

"Sure is…" But she was not getting a cat. Not now. Her life was in flux and she needed to remember that. Six months from now, she'd be starting over in Austin. If she still wanted a furry companion in January, she'd visit a shelter in Texas and adopt one then. There was never a shortage of cats needing homes.

The kitten wiggled in her arms, ready to get down. With a last kiss on its fluffy gray head, Mel let the little furball go.

More kittens ventured near. She petted them and laughed when they batted at her with their tiny paws and jumped about on the hay bale stacked behind the one where she sat with Gabe. A gray tabby fooled around at their feet, hopping into the spaces between their boots.

Yeah, okay. She really did like cats. They were cuddly and self-sufficient, the perfect pet for a professional woman. And every one of these kittens made her long to be a cat owner again. Especially now that she'd shed the cheating fiancé and his supposed allergies to cat hair. What, really, was stopping her from choosing a Happy Hearts fur baby for her own?

Gabe leaned in closer. His clean scent seduced her. "You know you're tempted," he whispered.

Tempted. That was exactly the right word. And not only when it came to the kittens.

But her job right now was to resist. No kitten of her own until she got to Austin. And no hot, not-so-lonesome millionaire cowboy in her bed, either. Now was her time to work hard for DJ, make plans for her new start in Texas and generally avoid anything that might in any way become an entanglement.

She met Gabe's eyes. "Not getting a kitten," she said patiently as they shared a long, way-too-intimate look that upped the temptation quotient by a factor of ten thousand.

"Whatever you say." He caught a lock of her hair and casually guided it back over her shoulder. All at once, she was breathless. The man was a menace—in the best sort of way.

He put his arm around her. She let him, even though she knew she shouldn't, that it would only encourage him.

And then she went even further and leaned her head on the hard, warm curve of his broad shoulder. "I'm really, truly not getting a—"

And right then, she saw him. *The one.*

A skinny little stick of a black cat with short, scruffy fur and enormous, spooky gray-green eyes. He sat very straight over by the viewing wall, his impossibly long, sparsely furred black tail wrapped around his tiny feet—and he was staring right at her.

How did she know *he* wasn't a *she*? Not a clue from this distance. But somehow, she did know.

With her head on Gabe's shoulder, his lean arm around her, Mel stared that wild-eyed black cat down. Neither she nor the skinny cat blinked.

Homer, she thought. *For some crazy reason, that wild-looking little guy reminds me of Homer.*

"Who's Homer?" Gabe asked.

She must have said his name out loud. "He's this old guy who lives in Rust Creek

Falls. Kind of a mystery man, you might say. He's in his seventies, at least, and probably older. He's likeable, really, and kind, too—but also weird."

The little black cat sat, calm and alert, his big eyes locked on Mel. She gave him a grin—and he rose on all fours and arched his bony back in a slow, luxurious stretch.

Gabe squeezed her shoulder. "Weird, how?"

The black cat came toward them in a slow saunter as Mel explained, "Homer makes moonshine. It's very special moonshine, the kind that somehow always has people shedding their inhibitions, often along with their clothes."

"Interesting."

"Oh, yeah. One time, he spiked the punch at a wedding in the town park. There was a Rust Creek Falls baby boom nine months later."

"You're not serious."

"Honest truth." The black kitten reached their hay bale and sat at her feet, gazing up. The look in those strange, sweet eyes said he was hers and she was his and she might as well just go ahead and learn to live with that. She said to Gabe, "Nobody really knows where Homer actually lives. He might pop up anywhere, most likely when you're least expecting him."

There was no point in kidding herself one second longer. She could not resist. She patted her lap. With a single "Reow," the little cat leapt to the hay bale, and from there to her lap. Purring now, he curled himself into a ball and closed his eyes.

She petted him in slow strokes for a minute or two. Then she lifted her head from Gabe's shoulder and met his eyes. "I'm adopting this one."

He didn't even say *I told you so*, just, "Let me guess. His name is Homer."

There were forms to fill out before she could take Homer with her. At Daphne's special animal farm, they didn't hand over rescue animals to just anybody. Mel paid for Homer's neutering, which had already been taken care of. The woman who handled the paperwork said he was estimated to be eleven weeks old. The time for various vaccinations was coming up and Mel would be seeing to those.

"Pet store, right?" Gabe asked when they—and Homer, in a soft-sided cat carrier Mel had bought from Happy Hearts—got back in Gabe's crew cab.

Mel hesitated. After all, the deal was just the visit to Daphne's animal sanctuary, and then he would take her home.

He must have known what she was thinking. "Why not?" he coaxed. "You need to outfit the little guy. Might as well get on that."

Really, he did have a point. "You sure you don't mind?"

One arm draped on the steering wheel and the other stretched out along the back of her seat, he countered, "Do I look like I mind?"

* * *

Homer was not a good traveler. He yowled all the way to the pet store. Mel couldn't bear to leave him alone in the truck, so she took him inside, propped his carrier in the baby seat of the shopping cart and wheeled him up and down the aisles with them. He didn't make a peep as they filled the cart with every cat necessity she could think of. Apparently, he liked riding in the shopping cart a lot better than in a fancy pickup. As soon as they got on the road again, he started crying. At least it was a short drive to her place, where she went straight to the manager's office to pay her exorbitant pet deposit.

Gabe helped her carry Homer's gear in. They filled the litter box and set out food and water bowls and the cat bed, along with a variety of toys. Homer christened the litter box, drank some water and clawed at the large scratching post/play structure Mel hadn't been able to resist. And then, after nibbling a few bites of kibble, he jumped right up on Mel's bed and settled in for a nap.

Gabe said, "I'm guessing that nice cat bed you got him is not going to see a lot of action."

She parroted what her mom had told her way back when. "It really is better for him to sleep in a cat bed while he's little."

The twitch at the corner of Gabe's sexy mouth told her he was quelling a laugh. "Okay, then. Good luck with that."

A long moment elapsed. They gazed at each other. It felt way too good, just staring at him as he stared at her. She was trying so hard not to let things go too far with him. What she needed to do was start steering him toward the door.

But honestly, he'd been amazing, taking her to Happy Hearts where she found Homer, driving her straight to the pet store, letting her take forever choosing everything Homer might possibly need. It only seemed right that she at least offer him a beer and maybe some nachos.

They ended up sitting at the little café table out on the balcony, chowing down on chips drizzled in nacho cheese sauce and sprinkled with olives and jalapeños. She was laughing at something he'd said when Amanda appeared on the balcony next door.

Gabe and Mel got up and joined her neighbor at the low wall where their balconies met. Mel introduced them.

"Amanda Jenkins," Gabe said. "Marketing, right?"

Amanda granted him a cautious smile. No doubt she was thinking of the other day, when she'd tracked down a certain "lonesome cowboy" online for Mel. "That's me."

"I've heard good things. You did that campaign for the Association. Great work—and you also do outreach for Happy Hearts, right?"

"Clearly, I have no secrets," Amanda said wryly. "And thank you. I like thinking my clients are satisfied."

"They are. I can testify."

"Gabe took me to Happy Hearts today,"

Mel said. "And I tried, but failed, to come home empty-handed."

Amanda's smile widened at the news. "Mel. You adopted a pet?"

"Yep. A kitten." Amanda offered a fist bump and Mel took her up on it. "Come on over and meet him."

"I would love to, but it's worktime. I just took five to stare at the mountains and clear out the cobwebs, you know? Gotta get back to it."

"Come over when you finish, then?"

"Definitely." She gave Gabe a jaunty little salute and then vanished into her apartment.

Mel stared after her, feeling simultaneously regretful and determined. Amanda's appearance was kind of a wake-up call. Somehow, the sight of her new friend had snapped her back to hard reality. She and Gabe were not and would never be a couple.

And yet, here she was, driving out to his ranch for lunch, spending her day off with him, sitting on her balcony with him, sharing a beer. Was she giving mixed signals, or what?

Slowly, she turned to him.

Judging by the expression on his face, Gabe had a pretty good idea of what she was thinking. "Worn out my welcome, have I?"

Right at this moment, she didn't like herself much. "I really think that we…" She thought that they *what*? She had no idea how to finish her own sentence. "I just don't understand what I'm doing, you know?"

His eyes said, *Yeah, you do.* But he kept his mouth shut.

She tried again. "I like you, a lot. I really do. But I've told you over and over this… whatever it is with us, Gabe, it's not going anywhere."

He answered cautiously. "All right."

"What does that mean?"

"It means I get it."

"I don't think so. If you get it, why do you keep asking me out?"

He took several endless seconds to answer. She was starting to wonder if he ever would when he said, "Someone very important to me once told me that if you have to ask, the answer's no."

Huh? "Well, then why do you keep asking?"

Staring down at his boots, he raked at his spiky hair with a big hand. "Yeah. Not what I was getting at. It means that when you've met the right person, you just know it."

The right person? Where did that come from? She couldn't help blinking at him, baffled—and suspicious, too. "Gabe, we've known each other for a little more than a week. How can you possibly know I'm somehow the 'right' person?"

"Because I didn't have to ask."

"Ask *what*, exactly?"

"Mel." His eyes were warm, full of dangerous affection. "I think you know what."

How did he do it? He stood there before her, all tall and strong and smart and kind and generous. And handsome. Way too handsome. He could break a woman's heart so easily, tempting her until she said yes, and then letting her down.

He probably wouldn't mean to disappoint her. But that wouldn't matter. She'd be wrecked all over again.

She didn't need any more heartbreak, thank you very much.

"You're being purposely vague," she accused.

"And you've had enough for one day." He headed for the slider and pushed it open, stepping through into her apartment and striding straight for her front door.

She trailed after him, wondering what exactly was happening, wishing he wouldn't go, yet knowing that his leaving was exactly what she'd asked him for. "Gabe, I just don't understand you…" *Or myself, for that matter.*

He grabbed his hat off the small table by the door. "I think we're done for now. I had a good time today. I'll see you tomorrow."

"Huh? Tomorrow? I don't—"

"DJ's as usual, probably around seven."

"You're not listening to me."

"Yeah, I am. And I hear you, loud and clear."

"Gabe, we have to stop this. You just need to stop asking and I need to say no and mean it…" By then, she was speaking to the door as it closed quietly behind him.

Chapter Four

"I think you like him. And there is noth-ing wrong with that." Amanda, lying on her side across the bed, dangled a feather on a wand for Homer. The wild-eyed little cutie lay on his back, furiously batting at the feather as she lowered it teasingly and then jerked it away.

"What's *wrong* is that my plan is not to like *any* guy. Not for at least a hundred years."

Amanda chuckled as Homer managed to grab the feather in all four paws. He chewed at it madly, front paws clutching, back paws kicking, until she gave it another sharp tug and he lost it again. "Yeah, well. Good luck with that."

"You said yourself he's a heartbreaker, dating lots of women, never getting serious with any of them."

"Maybe heartbreaker was too strong a word. Face-to-face, he comes across as a great guy. And besides, you're not looking for anything serious anyway, are you?" Homer gave the feather one more good swipe, bounced to his feet and darted off the end of the bed. "Love your cat, Mel."

"He's a handful." Mel scooped him up off the floor and nuzzled his neck. But Homer was a busy guy. He squirmed and she let him go. He leaped from her lap and went to give his scratching post some serious attention. "Back to Gabe."

"I'm just pointing out that he seems like a great guy and it's beyond obvious he's gone on you. You ought to seriously consider giving the man a break."

"I'm confused. Weren't you the one who

looked him up online and then warned me off him?"

"I just provided information. Yeah, he's been out with a lot of girls. He's considered local royalty. Everyone wants to date the prince, right? Especially if he's tall and hot and very, very charming."

"I don't need that kind of trouble."

"Mel. You like him. It's obvious—and it's not a crime to like a guy. Okay, he's never been married. Maybe he just hasn't met the right woman yet. Would you give him a chance if he was divorced?"

"Why are we talking about this?"

"Think about it. It wasn't me who just said *back to Gabe*. Maybe he's like you and doesn't plan to get serious for at least another century. Why is that okay for you and not for him?"

Mel couldn't help laughing. "Whose side are you on, anyway?"

"Yours, of course. The Prince of Bronco has a thing for you. Why shouldn't you enjoy him while it lasts? Nothing wrong with a great rebound."

"A rebound?"

"You need to look it up?"

Mel executed a blatant eye-roll. "I know what a rebound is. Too bad I can't say whether it's a good thing or a big mistake, since I've never had one."

"Hey, me neither." Amanda gave Mel a look from under her lashes. "But lack of experience has never stopped me from having definite opinions."

Mel found herself thinking how easy things were between her and her neighbor—both of her neighbors. Brittany as much as Amanda. She'd known the two women for exactly a week, yet it felt like she'd been friends with them all her life.

Amanda went on, "When you take advice from me, consider the source. I spend too much time online. In my spare time, I read a lot. I'm kind of rusty at real life. And that's the thing. See, I Internet-stalked Gabe for you when maybe I shouldn't have.

Nothing I found online was really that bad. And in person, I like him."

"I like him, too."

"I noticed. And it's because you like him that you keep letting him convince you to hang out with him. There is nothing wrong with hanging out with him. Why make it so complicated when it really isn't?"

Gabe spent Friday rounding up strays in a couple of far pastures on the Ambling A. It cleared his head to work out on the land, to play the ordinary cowboy he'd originally let Mel think he was.

Mel. He couldn't stop thinking about her, going back and forth like a damn seesaw, telling himself he ought to do what she'd asked him to and leave her alone.

Except...

Those jewel-blue eyes of hers told another story altogether. They said he shouldn't give up, that eventually she would give him a chance, offer him a little trust. Invite him in and *not* turn right around and ask him to go.

He should talk to Gramps about her. And he would, soon. He tried to get out to Snowy Mountain Senior Care at least once a week. It would be good to have a long heart-to-heart with the great-grandfather who'd been his idol since he was old enough to toddle around after him in diapers.

Nowadays, Gramps didn't answer much when Gabe talked to him. Advanced dementia made him unresponsive much of the time. Still, Gabe wanted to believe that Gramps was listening, taking everything in, mulling it over in that careful, serious way he used to have. Now and then, Gramps *would* answer back. But even when he never said a word, it always did Gabe good just to sit with him. Gramps had always been the one Gabe could tell his troubles to. That hadn't changed.

So, yeah. Sometime in the next few days, he needed to get his ass over to Snowy Mountain Senior Care.

As for the irresistible Ms. Driscoll, he would be there at DJ's Deluxe tonight just as he'd promised her—or maybe warned was more like it. He needed to give it one more try with her. Maybe she wasn't the one Gramps had always said he would find someday. But there was still something about her that made it really hard to walk away.

It was after nine when Gabe arrived at DJ's. Friday night in a popular restaurant tended to be busy, so he'd waited to come in until things were likely to have quieted down a little.

He wanted some face time with Mel, to tease her a little and have her give it right back to him the way she had the other times he'd dropped in to see her at work. Also, he needed a quiet moment when he took his best shot at finally coaxing her into an actual date. He wouldn't get that shot if she was running around dealing with the hundred-and-one things that needed her attention during the dinner rush.

There was one other reason he came in later than before. He kind of enjoyed the idea of making her wonder if he was going to show up at all. She kept saying he needed to stop chasing her. Fair enough. Let her suspect for an hour or two that he'd taken her word for it and given up on her.

Was he a fatheaded, entitled SOB to imagine she cared whether he showed up or not? Pretty much. But the way he saw it, he *knew* she cared. Showing up later might give her a nudge toward realizing that.

His stool at the bar was taken when he walked in. He found that kind of annoying at the same time as he grinned at his own damn ego to expect a certain bar stool to be there, empty and waiting for him, whenever he wanted it.

But then as it turned out, he was not only an entitled SOB but also a lucky one. As he scowled at his occupied stool, the woman sitting on it and the guy next to her got up and left. He sat down and the bartender served him his usual whiskey, neat.

He hadn't eaten since noon and was looking over the menu, trying to decide between a T-bone and DJ's famous ribs, when the woman he'd been waiting for spoke from behind him.

"I was beginning to wonder if you'd changed your mind about stopping by tonight."

He turned on his stool and—bam. Just the sight of her hit him like a shot of adrenaline straight to the heart. Tonight, her black skirt clung to her curvy hips and flared out around the hem. Her white shirt was tailored, pintucked to fit her snugly, showing off her little waist and the round perfection of her breasts. The undone button at the neck hinted at everything he hadn't seen.

Yet.

"Miss me?" he asked.

"Was that your plan?"

"My great-grandma Cora always said it's

not nice to answer a question with a question."

She tipped her blond head at him, considering. "So it *was* your plan."

"Maybe." He held up his thumb and forefinger with a half inch of space between them. "Just a little. Did it work?"

Her gorgeous smile bloomed wide. "I'm not even going to answer that one."

Right then, the restaurant's assistant manager appeared from the hallway that led to the kitchen. She signaled Mel.

"I'll be back," Mel said.

"I'm counting on it."

Twenty minutes later, as he was polishing off his appetizer, she reappeared. He asked how Homer was settling in.

She shared some of the little guy's crazy antics and admitted that she'd let the kitten sleep with her last night. "It's not like I have much of a choice. I put him in his bed and he jumps right out and leaps to *my* bed. It's a studio apartment. What am I going to do? Lock him in the bathroom?"

"That is a puzzler…"

She folded her arms under those breasts he was trying hard not to overstare at. "I know what you're thinking."

"You might be surprised. Hint. It has nothing to do with that crazy little cat you adopted."

She tried to look disapproving, but then ended up laughing. He laughed, too.

And then she was gone again, off to deal with some minor crisis or other.

She came back as the bartender served him his T-bone. "Looks good."

"Want a bite?"

"I'm tempted. But not while I'm working. It's not done for the manager to eat off the customer's fork."

"I would tell you to make an exception this once. But I know you won't."

"You're right—and please. Eat. Don't you dare wait on my account."

He leaned a fraction closer and lowered his voice to a slightly more intimate level.

"I don't mind waiting. Not as long as I'm waiting for you."

She didn't say anything. The bloom of color in her soft cheeks and the shine to her eyes spoke for her.

He took his time cutting a bite of his steak, chewing it slowly. "Excellent, as always," he said once he'd swallowed.

"That's what I want to hear."

"I liked your friend, Amanda."

"Isn't she terrific? She's got a roommate, Brittany. I feel like I've known them both forever."

"Brittany Brandt? Works for Evan Cruise and his Bronco Ghost Tours?"

"That's the one. But Brittany and the ghost tours have parted ways. She's got a job with Bronco Heights Elite Parties now. She loves it so far." Mel tipped her head to the side, thinking. And then she said, "It means a lot to have friends in a new town." She looked really sweet when she said that, kind of innocent and vulnerable.

"I'm sure it does. You might discover you

love Bronco so much, you can't leave in January, after all."

She gazed at him steadily now. It was as if they could have whole conversations while just standing there, staring at each other. He liked that about her—liked it a lot. That feeling of connection that went deeper than words.

But then she did speak and the words weren't encouraging. "I'm leaving at the first of the year, Gabe. A new start with a great job in a whole new place. It's what I need, it really is."

He wanted to argue that Bronco was better and if she wanted a job in finance and insurance, he could see that she found the right one here in town. But he didn't. January, as he was constantly reminding himself, was a long way away. "Got it. When's your next day off?"

"Tell me you're not going where I think you're going."

"What day are you off next?"

"You're like an EF5 tornado, you know

that? Relentless. Mowing down every objection in your path, all while looking like sin on a stick, with that easy, confident smirk on your face."

Sin on a stick? That meant she thought he was hot and that was just fine with him. He wasn't a smirker, though. Was he? *Stay on task, man. She's softening.* "What day?"

"Fine. Monday."

"Works for me. Dinner. I'll pick you up at seven thirty."

She gave him another of those long, speaking looks, after which she finally said, "Okay. Have it your way. Seven thirty." He barely had time for a mental fist pump before she added, "Now, eat your steak. I've got a restaurant to run." He watched her walk away, a perfect, petite dynamo of a woman, slim shoulders held proud and straight, curvy hips swaying.

She didn't come back. But that was okay. He smiled to himself all through his solitary dinner and allowed himself a second whiskey, as well. He figured he had a right to celebrate.

Mel Driscoll had agreed to an actual date with him.

Monday evening, Mel answered the door in a short, sleeveless dress of cream-colored silk. The silk was covered in lace the dusky purple color of the rose of Sharon that Gabe's mom grew in her back garden. That dress had a nice, deep V-neck and her shoes were a mile high, showing off those strong, sleek legs of hers.

Unfortunately, she had all her emotional walls back up again. Her first words were, "I can't believe I said yes to you."

He whipped out the fistful of sunflowers he'd picked up at a flower shop on his way over. "You look beautiful."

Her stern frown vanished and she sighed. "And you are much too handsome. Plus, I love sunflowers." She accepted them from his outstretched hand. "Thank you—and

you'd better get in here before Homer real-
izes the door is open."

Inside, she brought down a pitcher to use
as a vase as Gabe pulled out one of the two
chairs at her tiny table. The moment his butt
hit the seat, Homer leaped to his lap. "Hey,
little guy. What's up?"

The kitten stared at him through those
perpetually astonished gray-green eyes and
was silent. He allowed Gabe to pet him for
about twenty seconds. Then he shot to the
floor and attacked his scratching post.

Mel put the pitcher of cheery yellow flowers in the middle of the table. "All set." She
grabbed her small purse and off they went.

"The Association," Mel said as Gabe
rolled his Cadillac CTS-V to a stop in front
of his club. "I've heard about this place."

The valet, in black dress pants, a dressy
red Western shirt and string tie, pulled
Mel's door open and tipped his hat at her.
"Welcome."

"Thank you."

To Gabe, he said, "Mr. Abernathy, how are you?"

"All good, Jack. How *you* doin'?"

"Can't complain, sir." Jack ushered Mel out and shut the door, after which he ran around to Gabe's side and opened the driver's door. "You have a good evening, now."

Gabe got out. "I will, thanks." Once Jack drove away, Gabe went to Mel and offered his arm.

She took it as the Cadillac disappeared behind the sprawling clubhouse of wood and natural stone. "What happened to your ginormous pickup?"

"It's at the ranch. I like the Caddy now and then." He bent to her. "Is that a disapproving expression you're wearing?"

She stole his breath with a dazzling smile. "Not at all. That Cadillac is perfect for a night like tonight."

Pleasure stole through him, just to have won her smile. "Come on. Let's go in."

* * *

Mel found the Association clubhouse every bit as impressive as Amanda and Brittany had hinted it would be.

A pretty dark-haired woman greeted them in the foyer with its high beamed ceiling. "Gabe. So good to see you. Right this way."

She led them through a series of lounges filled with oversized leather sofas, dark wood tables and fine craftsman lamps with mission-style glass shades. Men and a few women greeted Gabe with nods and waves as they went by.

Giant, heavily framed windows looked out on the shadows of the high mountains in the distance. Closer in, the gorgeous landscaping was lit by in-ground lanterns. Every room had a stone fireplace large enough to roast a side of venison, each one with a rustic wood mantel the size of a tree trunk, much like the one in Gabe's living room on the Ambling A.

The woman led them onward, through the lap of rustic luxury that was the bar area and the main dining room to a private room with just one table. The window on one wall had the usual gorgeous mountain view.

"Thank you, Ariana," Gabe said after they'd been seated. As she went out, an old man came in. He wore a Western-style tuxedo and reminded Mel faintly of the butler in *Downton Abbey*.

The old guy greeted Gabe warmly, poured them water from a crystal carafe, took their drink orders and rattled off the dinner choices. Gabe asked for a couple of appetizers and the old man left, returning quickly with their drinks.

When he left again, Gabe said, "Rex has been here for as long as I can remember. He moves a little more slowly than he used to, but he takes great pride in doing the job right."

"I can see that." Mel sipped her lemon drop cocktail. It was perfect, both sour and sweet. "You know, a girl could get used to this kind of luxury."

Those chambray-blue eyes gleamed. "That's what I'm talkin' about." He leaned in across the table. "You're too far away."

For that, she gave him a one-shouldered shrug and surprised herself by suggesting, "Then move closer." The words got out before she could edit them.

Not that she really wanted to take them back, anyway. Gabe was a great guy. Why shouldn't she thoroughly enjoy every moment she spent with him? She'd made it way more than clear that whatever happened between them could only be temporary and he didn't seem the least concerned about that—and why should he be? So far, he'd shown no inclination in his own life to find the perfect woman and settle down.

And as for moving closer, he didn't need to be invited twice. Sliding his elaborate place setting to the head of the table, he took the chair in front of it. She scooted her own chair toward him. Now they were just around the corner from each other, in easy whispering distance.

Not that they really needed to whisper. It was just the two of them, cocooned in this beautiful little room.

Rex uncorked a bottle of wine and filled their wineglasses. He served their appetizers and left them alone for a long, sweet time.

They spoke of their childhoods. Mel explained that she'd always wanted a little sister or brother. "But not desperately. I also liked having my parents' undivided attention. I was kind of spoiled and that suited me just fine."

He said his dad was strict. "But my mom's a pushover. And when I needed a man to talk to, there was always my great-grandfather. Gramps taught me most of what I know about horses and cattle." He grinned. "Not that my dad didn't try. He and I just always ended up butting heads, somehow."

Their entrées appeared. Once Rex had left them again, Mel asked, "What's your sister like?" She was watching Gabe's face and saw the slight frown that creased his brow. "You…disapprove of Erica?"

He sat back away from her. "What makes you think that?"

"I don't know. Suddenly, you're frowning. And you're tensed up. Right here." She reached out and brushed two fingers between his eyebrows. It felt good to touch him. Maybe too good. She started to pull her hand back.

"Don't." He caught her wrist. His grip was firm and warm, the skin of his palm and fingers a little rough. Suddenly, her breath was all tangled up in her chest.

He pried open her fingers and pressed her palm to the side of his face. His warm skin was smooth, freshly shaven. Her breath hitched at the contact. "Don't be afraid of touching me, Mel. I like it when you touch me."

She felt thoroughly seduced, somehow, and tried to gather her scattered wits. "Wariness is not the same as fear."

"Why are you wary?"

"You know why. I don't think you really need to hear all that again."

"Do you want me to let go?"

Never. "Um, yeah. I think you'd better."

He turned his head just enough to touch his warm, soft lips to her palm. Heat skated along her arm, flared across her shoulder and up over her throat. Only then did he release her.

Rex appeared again to ask if they would like dessert and coffee. They both said yes and he brought them a decadent chocolate mousse to share. Mel enjoyed every bite and then settled back to sip her coffee.

Gabe said, "You asked about my sister..."

"I did, yes."

"She's completely absorbed in her life in Denver, with a longtime serious boyfriend and a great job in a growing company."

"Sounds pretty good to me." A lot like her own life in Bozeman—until Cheating Todd showed his true colors.

"Yeah." Gabe seemed a little sad now. "If she'd only come home every once in a while. She's been in Denver for twelve years, and every year we see less of her. We lost Great-Grandma Cora five years ago. Erica barely made it home for the funeral. My great-grandfather is not well. This is my sister's last chance to spend some time with him while he's still around."

For once, Mel was the one reaching out. She took his hand and wove their fingers together. She needed the contact—to show him support. "Hey..."

"Yeah?" He leaned closer, blue eyes warm as a bright summer day.

Drawn by the clean, intoxicating scent of his skin, she leaned in, too. "Cut her some slack," she whispered in his ear.

"Good advice," he answered ruefully.

"And sometimes that's the hardest kind to follow?"

"Yeah, pretty much..." He brought her hand to his lips and pressed a tender kiss to the back of it. She didn't pull away.

Was she sending the wrong signals? Probably. But this little room tucked away by itself seemed like a place where real life couldn't touch them. Where she could forget all the reasons she shouldn't let herself get too close to Gabe. She liked him so very much.

Every moment she spent with him just made it more difficult to remember why those reasons even mattered. It grew easier and easier to imagine crossing the line between a carefully controlled friend zone and something more.

More. It didn't have to mean forever, did it? When, in her whole life, had she ever taken a chance on having a little fun with a guy, having it be just for now?

The answer to that was a big, fat *never.*

Before her parents died, she'd known she wanted what they had—a loving relationship with a life partner, the kind of relationship that weathered the years, and children to cherish together. She would find a man she could count on, one who could count on her in return. Along with the right man, and the children he would give her when the time was right, she intended to have an interesting and challenging career.

After she lost her folks, she still wanted those same things, but even more so. Without their steady love and unwavering support, she'd felt cast adrift. Untethered. She'd needed to ground herself, to carve out a place for herself, make a new family after losing the family she'd loved so much.

By the time she'd said yes to Todd's marriage proposal, she'd been absolutely certain that he was the right man, the one she was meant to share her life with. The one she could count on to cherish her and love her as she would cherish and love him for the rest of their lives, the one she could trust to have children with.

And then Todd blew her trust all to hell.

Was there really any coming back from that for her?

Maybe not.

Not every woman ended up half of a couple with children around her. She might just be destined to go it alone.

What if that ultimately turned out to be the case for her?

The thought that it might caused a deep, echoing sadness within her, as well as a need to reach out and grab hold of the good things. She was no longer waiting for *the one*. And tonight, with Gabe, she couldn't stop asking herself a different kind of question.

Why couldn't she have something wonderful just for now?

She glanced down into her empty coffee cup.

Gabe asked, "More coffee?"

She sent him a grin. "This was perfect. Nothing more, thanks."

A few minutes later, they waved goodbye to the pretty hostess in the front foyer and went out into the summer darkness where the Cadillac was waiting.

"Come out to the Ambling A with me," he offered as they left the Association behind. "Just for a little while."

It had been such a great evening. She really didn't want it to end. And she didn't have to be at DJ's until late afternoon to-morrow. "All right. I would like that."

"Where's Butch?" Mel asked as Gabe ushered her in the front door. "I thought he'd be right here waiting at your door."

"He's over at the other house. He likes to hang out with Malone and my folks when I'm not around. They spoil him rotten, not that I mind." He led her into the big living room. "Brandy?"

"Brandy sounds just right."

He tapped at his phone and music played. It was country, a slow song. They settled on the sofa. She sipped her brandy, enjoying the warmth and the heady flavor.

"It's so good," she said. "This evening. The dinner. This brandy…you."

He set his glass on the beautiful burled wood coffee table in front of them, then gently took hers from her hand and set it down, too. She didn't object. She was much too eager to find out what would happen next.

And she was not disappointed.

He touched her cheek and then traced her jaw, his big, warm fingers sliding under the waves of her hair to gently cradle the nape of her neck.

"Melanie." He said her given name rough and low, lingering over it, as though savoring the taste of it. She preferred to be called Mel. It was short, sweet and strong, and that was how she saw herself. But tonight, well, the way he said her full name worked for her in a big way. "All night, I've been hoping I might just get a chance to do this..."

He gathered her into him. For a long, sweet span of seconds, she was looking in his eyes, feeling lazy and easy, arousal curling through her, smoky and warm as the taste of the brandy on her tongue. Then he covered her mouth with his.

She let her eyes drift shut as she opened for him. The kiss bloomed into something hotter, more urgent, as his tongue swept in to taste her.

Beneath his crisp white shirt, his broad

chest was hard and hot to her touch, and his arms held her so tight, like he would never let her go. Images danced on the insides of her eyelids—his smile that first day when they met out by the creek, the patient look he'd given her every time she'd told him no, those nights at DJ's when she would spot him at the bar as he glanced up and saw her looking his way.

Whatever this was, this heat and energy that always arced between them whenever he was near, she wanted more of it. She wanted it now.

He leaned back enough to capture her gaze again. "I'm thinking you really need to spend the night here with me."

Okay, yeah. She'd been thinking pretty much the same thing.

Pulling the trigger on that, though—it was another big step altogether. "Really not sure that's such a great idea."

He kissed her, soft and quick. "That's okay. I'm sure enough for both of us."

She fondly combed his spiky hair back

with her fingers. It was silky to the touch. "I am so tempted."

"Excellent." That smile of his was downright combustible. "And you know what they say…"

She lifted up from her lazy slouch against the cushions to press a kiss to that sculpted jaw of his, lingering long enough to nip him lightly with her teeth. "Tell me. What *do* they say?"

"The best way to get over a cheating rich guy is to jump right in with an honest man."

"You mean someone like you?"

"That's right. You should jump right in with me, Mel. You should do that right now, tonight."

"You, the rich guy who pretended to be a poor cowboy when I met him?"

"We've been over that. Let's not go there again."

She laughed, the sound low and husky to her own ears. "But it's so much fun to razz you about it."

"Fair enough. Go ahead. Razz me all you

want, just as long as you…" He nuzzled her neck. "Stay." He breathed the tender word against her skin. "I want you, Mel. Here. In my arms. All night long."

And then his mouth found hers again and they were kissing, endlessly kissing. He slid a questing hand down her body, under the curve of her bottom and on along her thigh, over her short skirt to the bare skin midway to her knee. Every inch of her flared with heat and yearning in the wake of that long, slow caress. His palm skated lower, over her knee and down her calf. When he reached her ankle, he eased off her high-heeled shoe. She heard a soft *thunk* as it hit the floor.

The other shoe followed right after.

No doubt about it. All the so-valid reasons she had *not* to go where she was going with him right now were blown away. By his touch. By each and every teasing conversation she'd indulged in with him at DJ's in those evenings he'd shown up to sit at the bar. By the way he always looked at her as if she was the only other person in the room.

Right now, it didn't matter in the least where this might be going. She was swept away by his manliness, his great sense of humor, that burning look in his summer-sky eyes. Somehow, he'd done it, thoroughly seduced her. And tonight, she was ready to relax and enjoy this for what it was—the magic of true chemistry, the pleasure she might find in one perfect night with a man like Gabe.

There was no tomorrow. Only now. Only Gabe and his captivating kisses, his bold, burning touch. For once in her life, she was going for it, giving herself up to the delicious decadence of it, a wild night with the right man—not a man for forever, but the perfect man for right now.

And as for tomorrow?

Tomorrow could damn well take care of itself.

Chapter Five

Gabe couldn't believe it. It was happening at last.

He had Mel in his arms and he wasn't letting go.

He kept kissing her, greedy for her. He wanted to claim every inch of her with the heat of his mouth. She was eager, ready. Every signal she gave him said yes.

She clutched his shoulders and surrendered her mouth to him, moaning so sweetly when he kissed his way down the V-neck of her dress, into that soft, perfect valley between her pretty pale breasts. She urged him on with eager sighs and softly murmured encouragements.

"Yes," she cried low as he nibbled her collarbone. "Please," she begged sweetly as he swept her heavy, fragrant hair aside to get to the long zipper at the back of that sexy little dress. With a sizzling purr of sound, the zipper parted.

"Gabe. Anything, everything," she whispered as he pulled the dress down her arms, revealing a purple lace bra and more smooth, kissable skin.

He pressed his hungry mouth to the tiny satin bow between the perfect swells of her breasts.

She let her head fall back. "Yes," she said again, her long hair falling every which way, curling down her back, tumbling over her satiny shoulders.

He kissed his way up over the top rim of the lace, a chain of kisses, first one breast and then the other. When he couldn't wait another moment to uncover her, he undid the clasp and the bra fell away.

She stared up at him, open to him, her eyes a jewel-blue sea of want, of yearning. "Gabe," she whispered. "Oh, please. Yes…"

He took one hard, pebbled nipple and then the other in his mouth as she clutched him close, crying his name again, begging him, "Gabe, yes, more…"

More sounded very, very good to him.

But not here.

He wanted to stretch out with her. The leather sofa was a big one, but not big enough.

He tipped up her chin and she gazed at him dazedly. "Hmm?" she asked sweetly.

"Bedtime."

A quivery little breath escaped her. "Um. Okay."

Oh, he could get used to this side of her. So soft and innocent. Not the sharp and guarded Mel he sparred with at DJ's. This was a softer Mel. Vulnerable and yielding.

Rising, he caught her hand and pulled her up to stand with him. The skirt of her dress still hung around her hips. She glanced down over her bare breasts and then back up at him. "I guess I don't need this right now, do I?" And she pushed the dress down. It fell in a satin and lace puddle around her bare ankles, leaving her standing there in nothing but tiny purple panties.

He indulged in a long, slow look. At all of her, from her strong, slender legs to the outward curves of her hips, the fine indentation of her waist, the womanly beauty of her round breasts. There wasn't an inch of her he didn't want to kiss, to hold, to worship all night long.

Her hair spilled down over her shoulders, golden, wild and curling. She was glorious. A sight to behold.

"There." She stepped out of the dress, snatched it up and tossed it across the back of the sofa. Gently, she nudged her shoes with a toe until they were under the coffee table. And then she held out her hand to him.

He took it, but only to turn her and scoop her high against his chest. With a low, happy sound, she twined her arms around his neck and dropped a sweet little kiss at his jaw.

"Ready?" He kissed her plump, delicious lips, thinking of how long he'd waited. To find her. To hold her. He'd dated a lot of women, gotten himself something of a rep for never sticking with even one of them. Slowly, he'd reached the sad conclusion that Gramps didn't know what he was talking about. There was no special woman out there for him, no one who was *the one.*

Well, Gabe got it now. He was a believer. Gramps was right. With this woman, he didn't have a single doubt. He truly didn't even need to ask.

"Let's go," she said softly.

Cradling her close, he headed for the master suite.

In his room, he carried her straight to the bed, which was already turned down by the housekeeper who came in daily to whip everything into shape.

"Where are you going?" she demanded

when he gently set her on the white sheets and took a step back.

"Nowhere." He unbuttoned his shirt, impatiently enough that two buttons went flying. "I'm staying right here with you." He tossed the shirt at a chair, turned and dropped to the side of the bed to pull off his boots.

As he was tugging on the second one, her smooth, cool hands came around him from behind. "I like it better when you're close." She pressed her naked breasts to his bare back and the silky skin of her slim arms encircled him. For a moment, he forgot how to breathe. He felt her lips against his shoulder.

And then those clever hands of hers got busy unbuckling his belt.

He chuckled at that, turning his head to share a kiss with her over his shoulder—a long, sweet one. His eager tongue met hers, tangling. She moaned into his mouth. It was possibly the sweetest, hottest sound he'd ever heard.

The boots were off in a matter of seconds. Socks, too, as he kissed her. She undid his belt and whipped it away. Her nimble fingers dealt with his fly.

He hated breaking their long, sweet kiss. But it had to be done for him to get out of his pants and boxer briefs. He stood and shoved them down, groaning a little when his erection got in the way.

Finally, though, everything was off. He turned to her and his heart stopped. She'd dispensed with those tiny panties. On her knees on his bed, her hands on her creamy thighs, her golden hair all over the place, she was an invitation to sin. Those eyes were cobalt-blue right now, full of longing and secrets, deep and dark as a hidden pond in some magical forest glen. He loved the look of her, so small and strong and perfect, without a stitch on.

She caught her lower lip between her pretty white teeth, the way she did when she was uncertain. "Gabe. What's the matter?"

He gave her a slow smile. "Not a thing."

"You sure?" She was chewing on that lip a little now, adorable and nervous.

He bent, put a finger under her soft chin and used his thumb to pull her lower lip free. "If anyone's going to be biting those pretty lips tonight, it will be me."

At last, she smiled again. "You looked so serious there for a moment."

"You're beautiful." He kissed her quick and hard. "All of you. I'm very serious about that."

"Oh, Gabe..." She came up on her knees, reaching for him.

Best invitation he'd ever had. He went down to her, wrapping his arms around her good and tight, rolling her little body under him.

She felt like paradise, like she'd been made just for him.

They kissed, one of those kisses a man can get lost in, the kind where he hoped he would never be found. Her hair tangled around them, silky. Wild. And her soft hands stroked his shoulders and strayed down his back, pausing in the dip of his spine, rubbing there as she made the sweetest, softest, hungriest little sounds that echoed pleasurably inside his head as their endless kiss continued.

He wanted more—to get his mouth on every inch of her. She whimpered in protest as he broke their long kiss and then sighed in delight as he kissed his way across her collarbone and then back to that little notch at the base of her smooth throat.

From there he went down, stopping to worship each pink-tipped, round breast, and then moving lower, dipping his tongue in the tender well of her navel, but not stopping there.

Oh, no. He wanted—*needed*—to kiss the secret heart of her.

But he took a small detour first, down to the tender groove where her hip met her body. He kissed her there, pausing to scrape his teeth against the sweet jut of her hip bone. She stirred restlessly, making little pleading sounds that only got him more determined not to rush a single caress during this first time with her.

He began on the other side, lavishing equal attention there, too, as she begged, "Please, Gabe," and clutched at his shoulders, fisting her little hands in his hair.

Still, he refused to hurry. He lingered, nipping and kissing, so close to the feminine heart of her, but always, just barely, *not* there.

"Please, Gabe. You're making me crazy, you know that?"

He did know. And he was glad. Every moment with her was better than the last and he refused to miss an inch of her. She needed kissing all over and he was the man for that job.

He scattered a curving, twisting line of kisses down her to knees and over each shin. He kissed her pretty ankles and even the tips of her turquoise-painted toes. She begged all the harder, complaining that he was pushing her over the edge.

"I'll never come back," she cried. "I'll

just end up trembling in a corner chanting your name."

He chuckled over that. "Shh, sweetheart. It's going to be all right. Just be patient a little longer."

"Patient! You can't purposely drive a girl out of her mind and ask her to be patient while you're doing it."

By then, he was kissing his way back up the inside of her left leg, lingering on the tender inside of her knee. She moaned and cried out, encouraging him to keep moving upward. He did, slowly. So slowly...

When he reached the core of her, he lifted those slim legs of hers over his shoulders and settled in to enjoy the wet, musky taste of her.

She cried out sharply, grabbing his head between her clutching hands. And when she shattered, he stayed with her, using his fingers as well as his mouth, kissing her endlessly as her body crested, shuddered and then went limp and lazy.

A low, throaty laugh escaped her, followed by the sweetest little whimper of mingled satisfaction and disbelief. "How did you do that? That was… Oh, Gabe… I don't have the words. Get up here where I can kiss you properly." She was pulling at his shoulders.

He gave her what she wanted, easing her thighs back to the mattress, sliding up to take her in his arms again.

She grabbed his face between her hands and laid one on him, a long kiss, one that promised more pleasure to come. Then she rolled on top of him and rested her head in the cradle of his shoulder. "I think I'm going to need a minute or two to catch my breath."

He smoothed a shiny, wheat-colored curl away from her cheek. "Take as long as you need. We've got all night."

She sighed. "Homer will be pissed."

"He'll live."

She snuggled in a little closer. "At least I left him plenty of food, a full bowl of fresh water and a clean litter box. He should be fine."

He stroked an idle hand down the silky slope of her back and then traced her spine, set on memorizing her body, on learning every inch of the curvy, delicious perfection of her.

She sighed, kissed his shoulder and rubbed a soft hand up and down his arm. "You know," she said in a soft, happy tone, "I've never had casual sex before."

Casual—wait. What?

She went on blithely. "I can't wait to have more of it. I can really see now how this rebound thing can help push a person down the road to realizing she's truly over her cheating ex." She lifted up, stacked her hands on his chest and braced her chin on them. Those gemstone eyes gleamed. "So, thank you." She granted him her sweetest smile.

Gabe kept his game face on. He might be falling for her hard and fast and pretty damn deep, but he'd set himself up for where she was taking this. After all, an hour before, he'd been the one to suggest that the best way to get past what her douchebag ex had done to her was to spend a hot night with a man who would treat her right—namely, him.

How could he get on her for taking him at his word?

True, for him, this thing between them wasn't casual in the least. And her cheerful, offhand words hit him where it hurt.

But he needed to look on the bright side. He had her in his bed now. And no matter how lightheartedly she spoke of having herself some hot rebound sex, he knew she wasn't a woman who shared her body casually. This night was special. Someday she would admit that to him.

He could wait. Take his time with her. Give her plenty of space to come around to the real meaning of this night on her own. He cupped his hand around the back of her head and urged her up so their lips could meet. Closing his eyes, he lost himself in her kiss.

When he looked at her again, her eyes had gone hazy in the best kind of way. "Oh, Gabe…" And then she blinked and said hesitantly, "I forgot to ask…"

He knew the drill. "I've got a clean bill of health and condoms in the bedside drawer."

She gave a shy little laugh. "Me, too—on the clean bill of health. And I'm on the Pill."

"Then we're golden." He tugged her closer and covered her irresistible mouth with his.

After that, they didn't need words. He lavished kisses everywhere his hungry mouth could reach. And she sighed and pulled him closer, kissing him so deeply, her soft hands roaming everywhere.

When he pulled away long enough to deal with the condom, she stared up at him dreamily, so ready. So sweet. Once he'd rolled on the condom, she pulled him close again. Her hands moved over his skin, stroking him—down his arm, over his chest, as though she couldn't get enough of touching him.

He understood her need to have her hands on him. He felt the same about her. That he needed to be closer to her, to have his hands all over her, to lose himself in the scent and feel and taste of her.

Taking the lead, she pushed him to his back and eased one slim leg over him. She wrapped her pretty hand around him, held him in position and slowly lowered herself down to him.

They groaned together, eyes locked on each other, as she took him fully into her.

After that, things got frantic, desperate in the best sort of way. Hard and fast. Wild and out of control. He knew he would lose it, but somehow, he held on.

The rhythm changed, going deep, rocking long and slow.

He rolled them, so he was on top—and then rolled again. Face-to-face, on their sides, it went on and on.

Finally, she broke. He watched her let go.

It was the most beautiful thing he'd ever seen, the wild spots of deep color on her satiny cheeks, the hot flush rushing up her slender throat, the transported expression on her amazing face. He managed to wait for her to hit the peak before following her over the edge of the Earth.

Around midnight, as Mel was settling in, closing her eyes, drifting toward sleep, Gabe nuzzled her ear.

"I have a question." His deep voice set off sparks along her nerve endings, reminding her of the pleasure he'd just brought her— three times.

Clearly, she'd been missing out. Having sex with Gabe Abernathy was like no sex she'd ever experienced before. If this was rebound sex they were having, well, she never wanted to have any other kind.

Not only had Todd been a cheater, he'd been a slacker in bed.

But maybe she had been, too. Having sex with Gabe took sex to a whole other level for her. He not only did glorious things to her very willing body, he made her want to do fabulous, naughty things to him right back.

And she had. Oh, she definitely had. She could feel her cheeks turning pink just thinking about the things they had done. And she could not wait to do them all again.

She might be insatiable now. And guess what? She was just fine with that.

He was up on one elbow, grinning at her. "What are you thinking?"

She grinned right back. "I'll never tell. You said you had a question?"

"I do. What is your opinion of Ben & Jerry's?"

She levered up enough to kiss the tip of his nose. "Okay, now you've done it. Do you *have* Ben & Jerry's?"

"I might."

She poked at his rocklike, sculpted shoulder. "Now you're teasing me. It's not nice to tease the woman you've worn out with fabulous, hot sex, three times. A woman in my condition really needs some Ben & Jerry's. Any flavor—as long as there's plenty of chocolate in it."

He traced her brows with a lazy finger. "We'll have to get up and go to the kitchen, have a look in the freezer."

"I don't feel like putting my dress back on."

"Who said you had to?"

Five minutes later, they stood at the kitchen island eating Chocolate Fudge Brownie straight from the carton, sharing the spoon, Gabe in an old pair of jeans, Mel in his white dress shirt from earlier tonight.

Really, she was having the best time. Gabe was not only great in bed, fun to hang around with and generous and thoughtful to a fault, she just really, really *liked* him.

As he handed her the spoon again and she scooped up another decadent, delicious bite, she thought of the diary that had once belonged to a young man named Josiah, a young man with the same last name as

Gabe. That young man would be in his nineties now, if he still lived. He'd loved someone named Winona, who might or might not be the Winona Mel knew and admired. And what about the baby who hadn't died, after all? Was Beatrix still alive somewhere, in her seventies now? With no clue that the family she'd grown up in wasn't the one she'd been born into?

Mel had so many questions when it came to the diary and the heartbreaking story it contained. She kept telling herself to leave it alone, that it was none of her business, really, a mystery that would never be solved. And then, as soon as she denied the diary's hold on her, she would start wondering again, longing to find out what really happened to the young lovers and their child.

It hurt her heart to think of those long-ago lovers, lost to each other, so old now, or gone forever. Or to think of their baby, Beatrix, who could be anywhere now—if she was still alive.

"All of a sudden, you look so sad." Gabe

stuck the spoon in the carton and set the carton on the counter. He tipped her chin up with a finger. "What is happening in your beautiful head, sweetheart?"

Sweetheart. She could really get used to him calling her that.

"Hey, now..." He framed her cheeks with his big hands. One had been holding the ice cream. It was cold against her skin. "It can't be that bad."

"It's what you said, just sad, that's all."

His lips descended. He tasted so good— of cold chocolate and banked desire. She opened to him and the kiss went on for a while. Slow. Lazy. Tender. Achingly sweet.

When he lifted his head, he suggested, "Talk to me about it."

Did she dare? Before, it had always seemed somehow foolish to even go there with him or his family. If his family was the family who had fled her hometown in the dark of night decades ago, wouldn't he have mentioned it or at least looked uncomfortable when she'd razzed him about the

Rust Creek Falls Abernathys vanishing into the night?

She had way too many questions and very few answers. And the whole thing with the diary was a sore point with her. Wilder Crawford should have taken the diary back when she tried to give it to him. This was not her quest. She was a reluctant sleuth at best.

But then, well, tonight happened. Yes, she'd called tonight a rebound. But it didn't matter what she called it—tonight had changed things between her and this man who was turning out to be a whole lot more than she'd bargained for.

"I think you do want to talk about it, whatever it is." His eyes held hers, waiting for her to open up and explain herself.

"You might be sorry you asked. In fact, you'll *probably* be sorry you asked."

He gave her that smile, the one that made her want to move in closer and beg for more kisses. "Try me."

Standing there in bare feet, wearing only

his shirt, she shivered a little and wrapped her arms around herself.

"You're cold." He stroked a slow hand down her hair, smoothing it back over her shoulder. When she shivered again, he pulled her close. "I'll put the ice cream away and we'll turn on the fire."

They sat on the stone hearth right there in the family room off the kitchen. The fire there was gas. He turned it on with a remote.

"Better?" he asked.

The heat quickly soothed her. "Much." She met his eyes—and started talking. "A week before I moved to Bronco, I went to a wedding in Rust Creek Falls Park…"

Gabe listened, not once interrupting, as she detailed catching the bouquet, her encounter with Wren Crawford and the "gift" of Josiah Abernathy's diary that Wren had insisted she take. She repeated the information Wilder Crawford had shared with her, including the letter tucked away in the diary's binding. She explained her friendship with the old woman who had the same name as the girl to whom the never-mailed letter was addressed. She told him that she had gone as far as to check the archives of the *Rust Creek Falls Gazette*, where she'd found a picture of a young Winona that proved her elderly friend had been in Rust Creek Falls about the time the events in the diary had taken place.

She shared all of it, everything she knew about the long-ago love story and its tragic ending.

And when she was finished, he still didn't say anything.

In fact, he seemed…distant now. Far away from her, and much too quiet.

"Gabe?" She put her hand on his rock-hard bare arm. He didn't pull away, but it seemed to her that he stiffened. "Gabe. What's wrong?"

His eyes focused in on her face. "My great-grandfather…"

"The one you call Gramps, right?"

His head dipped in the slightest of nods. "Gramps's given name is Josiah. Josiah Abernathy."

Chapter Six

With the fire at her back, Mel wasn't cold anymore.

That didn't stop her from shivering, though, to hear that Gabe's beloved Gramps had the same name as the young man who'd written the diary.

Gabe was staring at her, his expression distant now, hardened. "Gramps was married to Great-Grandma Cora for seventy years. They had four sons together. They were devoted to each other. There was never any other woman in Gramps's life. My family has lived in the Bronco area for generations. No one's ever said a word to me about Gramps and his parents fleeing here from Rust Creek Falls for some shady reason having to do with this Winona Cobbs woman and a disappearing baby."

"You're angry."

"No, I'm not." He glared at her.

"You sure seem like you're angry."

He drew in a slow breath and then bent forward and braced his forearms on his spread knees. "Look. I'm sorry. I know I'm overreacting. But if Gramps *is* the same Josiah as in this diary you talk about, that would mean he's not the man I thought I knew."

She dared to touch him again. He let her take his hand. She held it between both of hers. He didn't try to weave their fingers together and neither did she. "Gabe, if your Gramps *is* the Josiah I just told you about, it was before he ever met your great-grandmother. It's not as if he had a secret life or he cheated on his wife or anything. The events of the diary happened over seven decades ago. Josiah was hardly more than a boy—a boy in love with a girl in a very different time than ours. He really did want to do the right thing. His parents were the troublemakers. You have to see that."

He pulled his hand from hers and raked at his spiky hair with his fingers. "I just don't believe that the Josiah in your story is my Gramps. I don't. It's a coincidence, that's all. A weird coincidence."

Mel felt terrible. She'd known she should keep her mouth shut about the damn diary. But no. She'd just *had* to lay it all on him and make him question the character of a man he'd always idolized—not to mention, his family's history. "You know, maybe it would help if you read the diary and the letter for yourself."

He turned those hardened eyes on her again. "Look, Mel. The last thing I want is to go digging for dirt on my family in some old diary some guy I've never met found in a ranch house more than three hundred miles from here."

She hard-swallowed at his cold tone. "I, um, understand." He turned and stared straight ahead. Anywhere but at her, apparently. She should get the message, she knew that. But she couldn't stop herself from making one more pass at the Josiah question. "You know, a conversation with your great-grandfather just might clear everything up. I would love to meet him."

He still refused to look at her. "You don't get it. The thing with Gramps is complicated."

"How so?"

Gabe shook his head. "He lives in a senior care facility. He's a fragile old man, far gone in dementia. He's withdrawn. Uncommunicative. Most times when I go to visit him, he doesn't speak. I can't tell if he even really knows I'm there."

"But maybe if we—"

"Mel. I'm just not comfortable taking you to see him, okay?"

"Um. Yeah. I get it. And I'm sorry. I should have just...let it be."

"It's not your fault. I encouraged you to tell me what was on your mind." His words were more than reasonable. But he still wasn't looking at her.

She really, really wished she'd driven her own car tonight. "I'm kind of thinking I've worn out my welcome here."

"No. Of course you haven't." He did look at her then, but not exactly with warmth.

"Do you think you could maybe drive me home?"

He stared at her. She dared to imagine he might urge her to stay. But then he only said, "All right. Let's get dressed."

The ride into Bronco Heights was anything but chatty. To Mel, the summer night, thick with stars, seemed empty and endless beyond the windshield.

Gabe pulled into one of the guest spaces in front of her building. She thanked him for the evening and tried to say good-night, but he insisted on walking her all the way to her door.

"'Night, Mel," he said when they got there. For a moment, she thought she might get a good-night kiss, that he was going to loosen up a little and leave her with hope that things would be all right between them.

But he only stared at her kind of wistfully for several awkward seconds, brushed her cheek with his warm hand and left her standing there trying to figure out how in the world such a beautiful evening could go so bad so fast.

Inside, she flipped on the light to find Homer sitting three feet from the door looking up at her through those buggy gray-green eyes of his. "Honey, I'm home," she said in a lame attempt at humor. Dropping her keys and purse on the table against the wall, she scooped up the little black cat.

He purred when she nuzzled that sweet space between his pointy ears. "It's for the best, I guess," she whispered to the kitten. "I mean, the last thing I need right now is another man in my life. I was getting in too deep with him, anyway." At the bed, she kicked off her shoes and stretched out on her back, resting Homer on her chest. For once, he didn't leap up and dart away, but settled in comfortably.

It was nice, feeling his purr right over her heart. Soothing. "We had a beautiful dinner at Gabe's private club. And then later, we had sex." Homer purred at her, his eyes low and lazy. "The sex was fantabulous. Even if it did all go to hell shortly thereafter." Homer stretched out a paw and batted at her chin. "Oh, really. Don't worry about me. I'm fine. Just fine."

She stared up at the ceiling, feeling kind of forlorn.

When Homer suddenly leaped to his feet and took off for his water bowl, she rolled to her stomach, wrapped her arms around her pillow and shut her eyes.

Gabe had said that Josiah lived in a senior care facility. It was probably right here in town. How hard could it be to track the old man down?

But no. That wouldn't be right, to go

against Gabe's wishes and snoop around behind his back that way.

However, there was no one stopping her from a little Googling of the local Abernathy family and maybe a visit to the Bronco library to have a look through the archives of the *Bronco Bulletin*. The Abernathys were an important local family. They probably got their names in the paper all the time...

The next morning, she looked around on the internet. Mostly, she just found current stuff about Gabe and his rather large extended family. There were several pictures of Gabe at local events, always with a good-looking woman on his arm. That was kind of depressing, actually. It was way obvious Gabe would have no trouble finding a pretty woman to take to dinner at the Association any time he chose to go.

She did find the obituary of Josiah's wife, Cora, from five years before. She'd died peacefully in her sleep at the age of ninety, after being married to Josiah for seventy years.

Nothing in that obituary made it impossible for Josiah to have been in Rust Creek Falls around the time that the author of the diary fathered a child with a woman named Winona Cobbs.

At a little past eleven, Mel headed for the library. In the archives of the *Bronco Bulletin,* she found Cora and Josiah's wedding announcement, complete with a grainy photo of the groom and his bride. Gabe's great-grandfather had been a tall, lean man with a serious face. Did she see a certain sadness in Josiah's eyes—or was that just her overactive imagination? The young Josiah looked a bit like Gabe, she thought, especially around the mouth and in the determined set of the jaw.

There were other articles that mentioned Josiah—at the baptisms of his four sons, the death of Cora's mother a few years later and the dedication of a new courthouse building fifty years ago. As a respected member of the Bronco community, Josiah had been asked to do the ribbon cutting.

Eventually, she ran out of hits on Gabe's great-grandfather. She started searching for information that might tell her approximately when the Abernathy family had moved to town.

No luck there. She also couldn't find a single mention of the Bronco Abernathys in the *Bulletin* until after the time the Rust Creek Falls Abernathys would have fled her hometown—not that that necessarily proved anything.

Mel left the library feeling kind of discouraged. A whole morning's work had brought her no closer to knowing if the Josiah in the diary might be the same man Gabe called Gramps. If she really wanted to find out what had happened to the Josiah of the diary, she should probably hire a PI or someone like Amanda who knew her way into all the nooks and crannies of the internet.

Mel was getting nowhere in the search for

the truth about Beatrix. And she felt awful about the way she'd left things with Gabe. That evening at DJ's, she felt anxious all through the dinner service. Her gaze kept straying to the bar, where customers came and went. But Gabe never appeared. What if he never contacted her again?

Just the thought made her heart hurt. Longing burned through her.

Seriously? What was the matter with her that she went moping around over Gabe? She had not come to Bronco to fall for a man. And if it was over with Gabe after their one spectacular night together, that was a good thing. Bronco was only a stop-over on her way to her new life in Austin, after all.

Still, she kept checking her phone. Not a call. Not a text.

Wednesday night was the same. No calls, no texts. No Gabe.

Thursday was her day off. More than once, she got out her phone and punched up Gabe's number. Somehow, she managed to keep her finger from hitting the call button. She kept herself busy, shopping for groceries, straightening up the apartment. She invited Amanda and Brittany for dinner that evening at her place. When the subject of Gabe came up, she waved a hand and said she really didn't expect to be seeing him again.

"What did he do?" Brittany demanded, instantly pissed off for Mel's sake.

Mel played it extra cool. "He's great, but it is what it is, you know? I like him, but I'm not looking for anything serious and I'm guessing he's not, either."

Amanda was watching her much too closely. "Translation—whatever went down, you don't want to talk about it."

Affection washed through Mel as she gave a low laugh. "You guys. How can you possibly know me so well in such a short time?"

"Seems like we've known you forever," said Brittany with an elegant shrug. "And you're still not going to tell us what happened with you and the crown prince of Bronco, are you?"

She shook her head. "I don't really want to get into it."

Amanda reached across the small table and gave her arm a comforting squeeze. "We're here and ready to listen if you change your mind."

Brittany picked up the bottle of red Mel had opened to go with the pasta. "In the meantime, you need another glass of wine."

Gabe somehow got through Tuesday without calling Mel. That night, after dinner, he joined Malone on the front porch for a couple of hours. They didn't talk much. After about half an hour, Malone asked what was eating him. He lied and said nothing. Malone gave him a disbelieving look, but at least the old man let it go.

Wednesday was harder to get through than Tuesday. Gabe almost convinced himself it would be okay to head over to DJ's and see Mel.

Somehow, he kept himself from going there.

Thursday, he woke up thinking he couldn't take it anymore. He *had* to see her.

By the time he'd had coffee and breakfast, he'd changed his mind. She'd probably want to talk more about that guy with the diary who had the same name as Gramps. Gabe just wasn't ready to go there.

Maybe he never would be.

And really, it was about damn time he paid a visit to Snowy Mountain Senior Care. He should've gone days ago. But first he'd been busy and then Mel had blindsided him with that crazy story about the diary and the missing baby and the star-crossed young lovers, one of whom had Gramps's name.

None of that justified his staying away. He owed Gramps a visit and he damn well would go. Today. No excuses.

North of Bronco Heights, Snowy Mountain was a rambling series of brick buildings surrounded by manicured grounds crisscrossed with walkways. The facility offered a full range of services, from independent living to end-of-life care.

Josiah lived at Snowy Mountain West, a wing of the complex devoted to seniors with varying degrees of dementia or Alzheimer's. It was a big, open building, easy to get around in, where Gabe's great-grandfather got round-the-clock care.

"Hi, Gabe! Right on time," said the chatty brunette behind the desk in the sky-lit foyer. "Josiah has been for his walk and he's chillaxing in the lounge."

"Thanks, Linda." He gave her a smile as he went by.

Gramps was sitting quietly on a big sofa, his watery hazel eyes focused straight ahead. Gabe greeted him and refused to be too disappointed when the old man gave zero indication he knew that Gabe was there.

"Come on," Gabe coaxed, taking Josiah's thin arm. "Let's go where we can talk." It only took a gentle tug and Gramps rose. Gabe tucked the wrinkled, heavily veined hand in the crook of his arm and led Gramps to his rooms, which were attractively decorated in blues and grays and included a living room, bedroom and bath. The living room boasted big windows facing a pretty stretch of lawn with a winding path and a lilac tree.

Gabe led Gramps to the sitting area, guided him down to the big recliner and took the love seat across the low table from him. Gramps rarely spoke anymore, so Gabe filled the room with the sound of his own voice. He talked of everyday stuff, some property he'd just sold for top dollar west of town and the going price of beef this year. He confided that he was still trying to convince his dad to let him try a small bison herd on the Ambling A.

"So far," he said wryly, "the old man says no followed by a big hell, no."

And then, well, he went ahead and got into the stuff Mel had laid on him Monday night. He said how it had really pissed him off that she could even suggest that Gramps might be the kid from Rust Creek Falls who'd filled a diary full of entries about some woman he called "W," whose full name turned out to be Winona Cobbs—a woman the young Josiah's parents did not approve of.

"This Winona person," Gabe said gently, "had a baby as a result of her love affair with the kid named Josiah. Then, when Winona thought the baby had died, she couldn't deal. She had to be hospitalized in a mental health facility in Kalispell.

"But a letter tucked in the diary said the baby, whose name was Beatrix, had survived. Beatrix is missing to this day—or so the story goes. Mel is very fond of a woman about your age in Rust Creek Falls whose name just happens to be Winona Cobbs. Apparently, the Cobbs woman isn't well and nobody has been willing to tell her what they've found out. They're afraid it might be too much for her to take."

Across the coffee table, a long sigh escaped Josiah. Gabe fell silent. He watched Gramps closely, hoping against hope that maybe today would be one of those rare days when his great-grandfather spoke to him, or even recognized him.

But the sigh was all he got. Other than that, Josiah didn't make a peep. He continued to stare in the general direction of a family portrait hanging on the wall across the room, one taken at least fifty years ago. It included Great-Grandma Cora and all four of their boys.

"I told Mel it couldn't be you, Gramps. I know Great-Grandma Cora was the only woman for you."

About then, Gabe realized he'd jumped right into the bizarre story of the diary without telling Gramps about Mel herself.

"And I guess you're kind of wondering who the heck this Mel person is." A nervous chuckle escaped him. "Her full name is Melanie Driscoll. I met her when she wandered onto the Ambling A not long ago. And since I've met her, well, I'm always trying to figure out ways to get close to her, you know? Last Monday night, I thought we were really onto something, Mel and me. Then she laid all this crap on me about the diary and the woman named Winona and the lost baby Beatrix and, well, I haven't called her since."

Gabe braced his elbows on his spread knees, linked his hands between them and stared down at his boots as he confessed, "But I want to call her, Gramps. I want to call her so much it hurts. With her, it's like you always said. I don't have to ask the question. When it comes to Mel Driscoll, somehow I already know. I'm in love with her, Gramps. She's the one for me." Stunned at his own words, he glanced up.

Josiah's eyes were empty. Gabe felt that emptiness echo in the center of his chest. He would have given the world right then to have Gramps look directly at him, to hear him say that he understood exactly how Gabe felt about Mel—or to set him straight if Gramps thought he somehow had it all wrong. Until the past few years, Gramps had always been the one to give Gabe exactly the advice he hadn't known he needed.

Now, though? Gramps just sat there, still and staring, making Gabe wish for the impossible—to turn back the clock, have a real conversation with the Gramps he used to know.

Gabe was halfway back to the Ambling A before he let himself admit what he'd just done.

Whether Gramps had heard him or not, he'd said it out loud.

He'd told his great-grandfather that he was in love with Mel.

And that scared the crap out of him. He'd never been in love before, not really. It had always seemed easy for him, to enjoy spending time with a woman, but not to get in too deep. He'd savored his freedom, maybe even felt kind of smug that he wasn't one of those guys who got his heart all tied in knots over a girl.

Gramps had always warned him that one day it would happen. That one day, he would finally meet the one for him and after that, well, he'd learn what it was to belong to another.

So was this it, then? This longing that wouldn't stop? This feeling of missing some big part of himself when he tried to stay away? This sense that he should be with her and the world wouldn't be right until he'd broken down all the barriers between them?

Damn. If this really was love, he wanted nothing to do with it. It had been one thing to pursue her relentlessly when he didn't comprehend the depth of his own feelings. Until today, the possibility that he would end up with his heart in pieces hadn't even occurred to him. After all, until now he'd never been with anyone who could leave his heart in shredded bits.

But now? Everything had changed for him.

For Mel, though?

Not so much.

She constantly insisted she was leaving in January. Even worse, the other night she'd made it crystal clear she considered him no more than a rebound, a diversion, a pleasurable way to thumb her nose at her cheating ex-fiancé.

She was leaving and she didn't take him seriously.

Where did that leave *him*, but with a broken heart?

Uh-uh. No way. He needed to stop moping around like a long-gone fool. He wasn't *that* far gone. Not yet. He needed to forget her.

And one way or another, he would.

Chapter Seven

Once again, on Friday night, Gabe failed to show up at DJ's. Mel hadn't seen him since their night out on Monday, the night they'd made perfect love—and ended up barely speaking.

He'd never even bothered to call or send her a text.

She was constantly reminding herself that his radio silence was for the best. But it didn't *feel* like the best. Not by a long shot. She missed him, damn it.

She missed him a lot.

And then she started thinking that maybe something had happened to him. Maybe he was really sick. Or what if someone in his family had been in an accident or something? And here she was thinking evil thoughts about him when life had thrown him a curve and he didn't know how to deal with it. He could be suffering. What kind of a friend would she be if she let him suffer without lending her support in any and every way he might need it?

And yes, she *did* consider Gabe a friend. They hadn't known each other long, but she liked him so much.

And she couldn't stop thinking about their one amazing night together. Really, they needed to get past her oversharing about the diary. If she'd upset him, she needed to know so that she could make it right between them again.

By Saturday morning, she'd had enough of not hearing from him.

She paced the floor as she discussed the situation with Homer.

"Really, what's the matter with me?" she asked the bug-eyed cat, who sat in the middle of her bed watching with that special look he had of startled interest as she marched back and forth a few feet away. "I'm not shy. I'm not afraid to call a guy I like. I'm not one of those women who waits by the phone but doesn't have the guts to take the lead and make the call herself." She halted, turned and glared at the kitten, who lifted a leg and started cleaning what was left of his man-parts. "So why have I been acting like some shy wallflower?" The cat rolled to his back and began chewing on his skinny black tail.

"Alrighty then, Homer. It's clear I'll get no answers from you." She marched to her small kitchen counter, grabbed her phone, punched up Gabe's number and held the screen toward the kitten. "If you don't stop me, I'm calling the guy now."

Homer said nothing. He did roll back over

and sit up, though. Low-eyed and lazy-looking, he just sat there and purred at her.

"So, then, I'll call him." She hit the call icon.

It rang four times.

And then, just as she was wondering if the damn thing would ever go to voice mail, he answered. "Hello, Mel."

"Gabe!" she said, way too loud and downright frantic. "Is everything okay?"

"Yeah. Sure." He sounded...beyond calm. More like bleak. Or possibly bored.

Her skin felt too tight, her face kind of clammy, and her heart pounded like she'd just run a couple of miles uphill. "It's only, well, I hadn't heard from you and I was wondering if you were okay and...everything." Inside, she was cringing. Could she possibly sound more desperate, more lame?

"I'm fine, really. Everything's fine." He did sound bored. Yes. Definitely. She was boring him.

"Okay. Well, great. I just thought I'd,

y'know, check in, thank you for the other night, which was beautiful—I mean, until I brought up the diary thing. If I've upset you with anything I said, I wish you would just tell me and let me try to make amends. I really didn't mean to be intrusive. Maybe I shouldn't have asked to meet your great-grandfather. I totally get why you're protective of him. I should have given the situation more thought before dragging an innocent old man into something that probably has nothing to do with him and might very well be a wild-goose chase, anyway. I apologize if I, well, stepped over the line, you know?"

"It's fine."

"Gabe." She wanted to reach through the phone and shake him—or maybe strangle him. "You don't *sound* fine."

"Look, Melanie…"

Melanie? It was down to him calling her *Melanie* now? That did it for her. "You know what, Gabe? Never mind. Just delete my number. Pretend we never met. You won't hear from me again. Goodbye." She disconnected the call.

She was standing there, vaguely stunned, feeling terrible about what had just happened, when the phone rang in her hand. For a fraction of a second, her heart lifted. She dared to hope it was Gabe, calling her back to apologize for acting like a cold-hearted jerk. But then she looked at the screen and the flare of hope died. She didn't recognize the number.

Answering calls from unknown numbers was rarely a good idea. But right at that moment, she was so upset over the way Gabe had just blown her off that she swiped up without thinking.

"Yes?"

"Mel. My God. At last."

"Todd," she muttered grimly.

"Oh, Mel. It's so good to hear your voice. I've missed you so much. Mom and Dad have missed you, too. I need you. *They* need you. Spurlock's needs you. The numbers have really dropped since you've been gone. It's bad. I'm a wreck. Mom and Dad are on my case. They love you so much, honey. *I* love you so much. Where *are* you, Mel? Up in Rust Creek Falls? I'll come to you, right away. If we could just talk, face-to-face, I'm sure you'll see reason and come back to me, to us, to the good life we've made together."

"Todd," she said again, taking great pains to keep her tone even and reasonable.

Todd let out a long sigh. "Ah. At last. There's my girl—yes, Mel. Anything. Whatever you want."

"I want you to quit trying to contact me, Todd."

"I can't quit. I *love* you."

"I *don't* love you, Todd. I'm not your girl."

"You're just saying that."

"Because it's *true*. Whatever I might have felt for you once, well, you killed that, Todd. Killed it stone dead. I am completely and totally through with you. I want nothing to do with you. When are you going to accept that it's over and move on?"

"It's not over. I need to talk to you. Just give me an hour, you and me, face-to-face. I'll make you see—"

"I've seen all I needed to see—a naked woman who wasn't me in our bed. With you. There's no coming back from that, not in my book. You need to let it be and move on."

"Just tell me where and when to meet you. Just let me—"

"Not a chance. It's over. Deal with it. I never want to talk to you again. I'm going to block this number and any other number you try to call me from. Stop wasting your time. Nothing you can do or say will change my mind. Give it up. Let it go. Move the hell on. Goodbye." She ended the call and blocked the number.

On the bed, Homer was still watching her. She sat down next to him. He rose from his haunches to crawl into her lap. She petted him slowly, soothed by the motorboat sound of his sweet purr. "Men," she said glumly to the kitten, since nobody else was there.

"When you're done with them, they won't go away. And when you want them, they're no longer interested."

Mel was wrong about Gabe.

He was very interested. And acting *un*-interested had been a bad idea. He realized that now. He'd freaked and tried to tell himself he needed to forget her.

Unfortunately, forgetting her wasn't happening. She filled his mind and heart.

So sue him. He'd never been in love before. He had a right to be bad at it at first. Didn't he?

Would Mel understand if he tried to apologize after not calling for four days, and then being a hopeless jackass when *she'd* called *him*?

No. She wouldn't understand. Why should she understand? Mel was a proud woman. She wasn't going to put up with a guy who treated her like she was wasting his time when she called to ask if he was okay.

He would hate it if she put up with a guy like that.

Even if the guy was him.

He'd lost her without having ever really had her.

What was he, thirteen again? He was certainly acting like it. Gone on a girl, being an idiot about it.

Disgusted with himself, he went to the stables and spent a few hours mucking out stalls with only his dog, the gruff head groom and the horses for company. The dirty job didn't improve his attitude any.

He returned to the house, cleaned up and put on a suit. He had a business dinner at the Association. Over good whiskey and a blood-rare porterhouse steak, he tried to keep his mind on the prospective project at hand: two blocks of luxury townhomes in Bronco Heights, which could be very lucrative for everyone involved.

But keeping his mind on business wasn't easy. His thoughts kept wandering to Mel. Had he totally blown it with her? If he showed up at DJ's again, would she even speak to him? If he knocked on her apartment door, would she refuse to answer?

He really didn't need a damn broken heart—and that had kind of been why he'd behaved so coldly when she'd called.

It was a case of seriously flawed reasoning. He was already in love with her. Being rude to her, trying to push her away, wasn't going to make his love go away. It only made *her* go away, which didn't help in the least.

He was miserable. Heartbroken already. And he'd brought it on his own damn self. He needed to do something to make things better, somehow.

Even if Mel would never give him a real shot at winning her heart, that didn't stop him from stepping up and apologizing for acting like a jerk when she'd been nothing short of a sweetheart, calling to find out if he was all right, trying to clear the air between them, wanting to let him know she wouldn't push him about the diary if he wasn't willing to go there with Gramps.

And as far as that whole thing with the diary, well, why not help the woman he loved clear up an old mystery if he could? What if the impossible turned out to be true and Gramps actually was the Josiah she was looking for?

Yeah, his first response to the story in the diary had been a defensive one—defensive for Gramps, for the family name, for the history of his family as he understood it.

But wasn't the truth supposed to set everyone free?

It had all happened decades ago. A baby had been lost, stolen from her rightful parents. What if that baby—older than his own grandfather now—still lived? What if he had a great-aunt he'd yet to meet who'd lived her whole life never knowing the family she'd been born to? What if a very old woman in Rust Creek Falls could be reunited at last with the daughter she'd lost at birth?

Gabe got home from his business dinner at a little after midnight. He felt edgy, uncomfortable in his own skin. For a while, he sat at his laptop in his study, trying to go over the numbers on the townhome project. His heart wasn't in it, though. He mostly just stared at the columns of figures and thought about how he'd messed up with Mel.

He didn't go to bed until after two.

And he was up before dawn. When he woke, he realized he'd made a decision.

Mel wanted to meet Gramps. And even if she was never going to let herself love him, Gabe loved *her*.

Real love equaled trust. And he needed to trust her enough to take her to his great-grandfather, to give her that shot at finding out the things she longed to know about the past. Whatever did or didn't happen between the two of them, Gabe could at least be the man who helped her get what she wanted.

But there was still Gramps to consider.

Would it be damaging to Josiah, somehow, to bring Mel to Snowy Mountain and let her quiz him about what could be the most painful secrets of his past?

Hell if Gabe knew. When he'd brought the subject up Friday, Gramps hadn't responded in any way—beyond a deep sigh, which might or might not have had anything to do with what Gabe was telling him. Chances were high Mel wouldn't get anywhere with the old man, either.

And really, what *did* Gabe know about his own family in the distant past, anyway?

Not a lot, now that he thought about it. Offhand, he couldn't even recall the names of his great-great-grandparents—on his father's *or* his mother's side. To him, the family history began with Gramps and Great-Grandma Cora.

Maybe he ought to start with lunch at the main house. He could ask his dad and grandfather about Gramps's parents and find out how the Abernathys had come to settle in Bronco.

Unfortunately, though the spread Malone put out was delicious as ever, information-wise, lunch was a bust. Both his dad and Grandpa Alexander said that the Aberna-thys had "always" lived in Bronco. Grandpa Alexander did at least recall his own grand-mother and grandfather. Josiah, Sr. and his wife, Noreen, had both passed away in their fifties.

"I hardly knew them," said Alexander. "They weren't the kind of grandparents who get down on the floor and play with the kids. They always seemed kind of dis-tant. And strict. We all had to be on our best behavior when Grandfather Josiah and Grandmother Noreen were around."

So much for learning about the family from his dad and grandfather. Gabe con-sidered approaching Malone, seeing if the cook knew anything. Malone really was like a member of the family, and he did seem to know things about the Aberna-thys that no one else had a clue about. But Malone had only been around for a couple of decades. To Gabe, twenty-plus years might seem like a long time. But the events that concerned him now had happened long before Malone became a fixture at the Ambling A.

Not knowing what else to do, Gabe decided to try again to talk to Gramps before taking the big step of bringing Mel to visit him. Maybe this time, his great-grandfather might show him some kind of sign that he heard and understood...

Gabe arrived at Snowy Mountain at a little past three that sunny Sunday afternoon.

Gramps was in the exercise room with several other residents. A fit-looking gray-haired lady led them through a simple routine of chair stretches followed by basic balance exercises and a few modified push-ups and sit-ups. Gabe waited near the door until the class ended. Gramps didn't really participate, but neither did some of the others. Nobody seemed to mind either way.

When the session was finished, Gabe led

Gramps back to his room, settled him in the recliner and took the love seat for himself.

He wasn't much encouraged that this visit would go anywhere. It was another of Gramps's "far away" days, as Gabe had come to think of them. Lately, most days were of the "far away" kind.

Josiah stared off toward the family portrait across the room, his eyes vacant, his expression unreadable. Gabe talked to him about everyday stuff to begin with, filling Gramps in on what had been going on with him since his last visit two days before.

Did any of it register with the old man? Hard to tell.

Gabe needed to keep his attitude on straight. If nothing came of this visit, so be it. He reminded himself that it was good, just to be here, him and Gramps. Together.

He leaned in. "I got a problem, Gramps. That woman I mentioned the last time I was here, the one I can't stop thinking about? The one who…" Why the hell was he stalling? He needed to just come out and say it, for God's sake.

He tried again. "Mel. Her name is Mel and I really am in love with her, Gramps. It's finally happened for me and I'm kind of freaked about it, if you want to know the truth. I'm in love with Mel and Mel has had a bad experience with a cheating douchebag ex-fiancé and she says she's through with men. She's got a job waiting for her in Austin at the first of the year. She says she's taking that job, moving on, not coming back. I'll probably have to learn to let her go, Gramps. Plus, I kind of treated her coldly when she called yesterday, which only made my chances worse with her."

Gabe paused for a breath and to judge Josiah's reaction. What he saw wasn't encouraging. Gramps was still staring off into nothing, his face an empty mask.

"Okay, so I'll get to the iffy part. I mentioned this last time, but just in case it didn't register with you, or whatever..." That sentence wandered off into nothing. He started again. "It's like this, Gramps. Mel has this idea that you're originally from her hometown of Rust Creek Falls. She thinks that maybe you loved a woman named Winona there, that Winona had your child and, somehow, Great-Great-Grandpa Josiah and Great-Great-Grandma Noreen arranged to take the baby, Beatrix, away from her mother and to arrange for a secret adoption."

Nothing. Zero response.

Josiah stared into space, same as Friday.

Who did Gabe think he was kidding? There was no point in continuing this one-sided conversation. He wasn't going to get any answers from Gramps.

He reached across the coffee table and gently clasped his great-grandfather's bony shoulder. "It's okay, Gramps. I love you."

It would be wrong to bring Mel here. Gramps was lost somewhere inside his own mind and he couldn't say yes or no to a visit from anyone.

Gabe got up, circled the coffee table and

bent to give the old man an awkward hug. Gramps sat passively as Gabe wrapped his arms around his thin shoulders, gave a gentle squeeze and then straightened. "I'm letting this whole crazy story go now. I won't bring it up again, I promise you."

Easing back around the coffee table, Gabe turned for the door. When he got there, he paused with his hand on the knob. "I'll be here again next week, just to check in, visit a little, see how you're doing." He pulled the door wide.

And right then, his great-grandfather said in a rough, rusty voice, "Don't give up on love. Bring her to me."

Gabe stayed for another hour. He spent the whole time trying to coax a few more words out of Josiah. He got nowhere. Gramps had reverted to a silent, staring shell of himself.

It hurt to give up, but what could Gabe do? He left reluctantly.

At the Ambling A, he sat at his desk in

220 IN SEARCH OF THE LONG-LOST MAVERICK

the study for a while, feeling kind of low about everything.

When he picked up the phone to call Mel, he wasn't at all sure she would answer.

She didn't. He hung up without leaving a message, though he was pretty confident she would call back if he admitted he was ready to take her to Gramps. A visit with Josiah was probably all she wanted from him now. And that grated.

Yeah, he had no one to blame but himself that she wouldn't take his call. He wanted to fix that—before he said anything about taking her out to Snowy Mountain.

And it had occurred to him that there was one solid clue he could probably track down as to when the Abernathy family might have first come to Bronco. He would follow through on that before trying to reach out to Mel again.

For the rest of the day, Mel constantly reminded herself that she was *not* returning Gabe's call.

He hadn't even left a voice mail. If he wanted to talk to her, he could damn well do her the courtesy of leaving a message, giving her at least a clue of what he needed to talk to her about.

But no. The prince of Bronco was above leaving voice mails explaining himself. He simply called and hung up and his loyal subjects fell all over themselves calling right back to beg for a chance to do his bidding. Whatever *that* might be.

She was buttoning up one of her many white shirts, getting ready for work, when her phone, on the dresser, pinged with a text. She was on it like a shot.

It was from Gabe: I was an ass when you called. I'm sorry. Give me a chance to explain myself?

Her shirt half-buttoned, her ridiculous heart doing something resembling a happy dance inside her chest, she stood holding the phone, her fingers itching to reply.

Nope. Uh-uh. Not happening. She dropped

the phone back on the dresser—and it lit up again.

Please?

Somehow, she managed not to grab the damn thing and start typing an answer. It was just better not to go there. They'd had one glorious night and she refused to regret that.

But as for giving him another shot, no. He was much too attractive for her peace of mind and he ran hot and cold. If she accepted his apology this time, how long would it be before he blew her off again?

She just didn't need that kind of grief.

"It's a minute of your time, Mel," argued Gwen. It was seven thirty that night. Mel and her assistant manager were huddled in the hallway between the kitchen and the dining room. Waiters and other staff bustled past them going in both directions, carrying orders and dirty dishes back and forth. "And he *is* Gabe Abernathy…"

"Of course, he is," Mel muttered angrily.

"Give the guy a smile and a quick hello. It's not going to kill you. You've had no trouble dealing with him the other times he's stopped by."

"Yeah. Don't remind me."

Gwen was frowning, confused at Mel's change of heart when it came to the Abernathy heir. But then she shrugged. "Okay. You're the boss. I'll tell him you're in the middle of something important and can't be disturbed." She turned for the dining room.

Mel grabbed her arm. "You know what? You're right. I'll talk to him."

Gwen hit her with a wide grin. "Excellent. I really wasn't looking forward to telling Gabe Abernathy that the manager didn't have time for him."

Mel emerged from the hallway and saw Gabe right where she expected him to be— at the bar. He'd already spotted her. As their gazes locked, a slow, gorgeous smile spread over that heartbreaker-handsome face of his. He wore a Western-cut jacket over a dark blue dress shirt, his spiky hair just begging her to shove her fingers in it.

She strode toward him with a rising feeling of pure anticipation. She'd missed him so much. The ass. "What can I do for you?" she asked, ladling on the irony, as she slipped into her usual spot between his stool and the next one over.

"Pick up the phone, for a start," he said downright tenderly.

She resisted the urge to fold her arms across her middle in a clearly defensive gesture. "I was reluctant to bore you, the way I obviously did the last time we spoke on the phone."

"You have never once bored me, Mel."

"If you weren't bored, then what?"

"Crazy 'bout you, Mel, and frankly scared of my own damn feelings."

Warmth stole through her. She stiffened her spine, but her anger had fizzled. She asked, a plaintive note creeping in, "Really, Gabe. What do you want from me?"

He answered without having to stop and

think about it. "A little while alone, just you and me. Somewhere other than here, someplace quiet, where we can talk privately." His eyes were steady on hers. She believed him, believed his sincerity in this moment, even though she wanted to wrap herself in a protective shell of doubt and suspicion. "Are you off tomorrow?"

Her throat felt tight. She gave a little cough to clear it. "I am, yes."

"Meet me at noon. On the Ambling A. Same spot along the creek where I found you that first day?"

There were so many reasons she shouldn't. But none of them mattered in the least—not against the hungry, deep beating of her heart and the longing she couldn't seem to shake. "All right, Gabe. Noon tomorrow, that spot by the creek."

He tossed some bills on the bar, got down off the stool and leaned in. His breath warmed her cheek as he whispered, "See you then."

She watched him walk away, so tall and

broad-shouldered, proud and strong. The last thing she'd planned to do was give the man another chance.

Yet, she'd agreed to meet him. She should probably be having second thoughts about that decision.

However, the mere sight of him had reminded her sharply that she really had missed him. It was hard to stay mad at him when every cell in her body yearned to be close to him again.

Chapter Eight

By noon the next day, when Mel pulled her Audi in behind Gabe's giant black pickup on the dusty ranch road, all her doubts had resurfaced. She really shouldn't be here, yet somehow, once again, she'd let him convince her they needed to...

What?

She didn't even know what this meeting was about. Some men were just plain dangerous to a woman's heart and mind and, well, general equilibrium. Gabe Abernathy was the premiere example of that kind of man. She ought to just start up the car again and drive away.

But she'd said she would meet him here and she was a woman who followed through on her commitments.

At least, that was the excuse she gave herself as she emerged from the car and climbed the dirt path that led to the spot by the creek under the cottonwoods where they'd first met. She crested the gentle rise of the hill and there he was, below her. He sat on a blanket beneath the dappled shade of a cottonwood, next to a picnic basket, facing the creek.

How was she supposed to stand firm against him when he showed up with a picnic—and at the spot where they'd met and shared their first kiss, no less?

Squaring her shoulders and reminding herself that she had to be strong, she descended the hill.

Gabe heard boots on gravel. Rising, he turned to greet her.

Damn, she was beautiful, in rolled-cuff

jeans that fit her curvy hips like a glove, those cute short boots she favored and a silky shirt splashed with a swirling blend of pink, purple and jewel blue. "Hi."

She stopped on the edge of the blanket. "Hey." Her gemstone eyes spoke of doubts and her plush mouth twisted down at the corners.

Refusing to feel the least discouraged, he offered a hand. She took it with obvious reluctance. He reminded himself that at least she was here, her hand cool and soft in his.

"Come on," he coaxed. "Sit down." She dropped to the blanket and he settled in beside her. A few feet away, Little Big Bear Creek burbled cheerfully. The sweet, high warble of a meadowlark rose from the wild grass somewhere nearby and Ambling A cattle grazed beyond the fence across the rippling ribbon of water. The sky was cloudless, an endless sheet of pale blue. No rain in the offing today. "Malone makes this chicken salad with grapes and pecans and all kinds of stuff you wouldn't think of when you think chicken salad."

At last, she gave him a smile. Suddenly, the world was a brighter place. "I love chicken salad with grapes and pecans."

"On crusty bread, with chips and a wine cooler?"

"Perfect."

He flipped open the basket and served her lunch. Except for the intermittent serenade of that lone meadowlark and the babbling of the creek, they ate in silence. As each minute passed, his feeling of dread increased.

He'd asked her to come here to the exact spot where they'd met so that he could tell her he'd fallen in love with her. But she held him at a distance with her careful silence. He had a sinking suspicion that a declaration of love from him right now would have her leaping to her feet and sprinting for her car.

Clearly, he needed to slow the hell down to baby steps with her. No sense in making his big declaration if it was only going to send her running for the hills.

"That was so good," she said, once he'd

put the remains of the food back in the basket. She took another sip from her wine cooler, carefully set the half-empty bottle on the blanket beside her and leaned back on her hands. Almost shyly, she turned those deep blue eyes his way. "So, um, you had something you wanted to talk to me about?" Her mouth was softly parted. He wanted to kiss her so bad, to wrap her up good and tight in his arms and never let her go.

But she gave off a definite vibe, one that said he'd better keep his lips and grabby hands to himself. "I can't stop thinking of our night together. I really have missed you, Mel. I want another chance. I want to spend more time with you."

She tugged at a loose thread on the blanket and dragged her gaze up slowly to collide with his. "Have you forgotten how you couldn't wait to get rid of me that night?"

"You have to know, that wasn't about you."

"You *acted* like it was about me. When I

tried to apologize for upsetting you, you said it wasn't my fault. But your eyes were cold and when I said I should go, you couldn't hustle me out the door fast enough."

He wanted to keep denying his own behavior, but he knew that wouldn't cut it with her. "You're right, about all of it. Will you let me explain?"

She answered with a half shrug. "Go ahead, then."

"It got to me, got to me bad. Just the idea that my family might have a whole other story I never knew a damn thing about, that my Gramps might have loved someone else before he loved my great-grandmother, that my grandpa Alexander might have a half sister he's never met. It was a lot to process and I did kind of blame you—you know, like that old saying. I wanted to shoot the messenger.

"I knew at the time I was in the wrong, but I wanted so bad *not* to know what you'd just told me. It was completely unfair of me, Mel, to blame you for telling me something

I didn't want to hear. And I really am sorry. I only hope that maybe you'll forgive me for being such a jerk about it."

For several uncomfortable seconds, she simply stared at him. And then slowly, she nodded. "Okay, yeah." The word was more breath than sound. "I do understand. It's hard information even for me to deal with—that the Winona Cobbs I know and love in Rust Creek Falls might have this tragic past she's never said a word about. Gabe, I didn't even *want* that diary. Lately, I feel like this heavy burden has been laid on me. I try to ignore it, but it nags at me, you know? The questions echo in my head. What really happened all those years ago? And did it happen to strangers—or to *your* great-grandfather and *my* Winona?"

He caught her hand. She let him, so he went further and wove their fingers together.

She held his gaze. She wasn't smiling. "You didn't call."

"No, I didn't. And that was wrong, too."

A humorless laugh escaped him. "And then *you* finally called *me*. You were so sweet."

"You weren't." She scowled at him.

"Most men are fools." *Especially when it comes to love.* He thought that last part, but somehow kept himself from saying it. "I'm sorry, Mel. I'm beggin' for another chance here, but I have to admit, if you say no, I can't really blame you."

She squeezed his hand. He told himself that had to be a good sign. When she spoke, though, he wasn't so sure. "I just… Gabe, I don't want to give my heart again. I really don't. My heart broke when I lost my parents. Todd broke it a second time. My poor heart just doesn't have another break left in it."

He wanted to swear he would never hurt her—but he already had, hadn't he? And as for the whole love thing, well, how could he bear to say he loved her when she'd just said she was through with love? He brought their joined hands to his lips and kissed her knuckles one by one.

His hope rose again when she leaned her head on his shoulder. He wrapped an arm around her, brushed his cheek against her silky hair and breathed in her perfect scent of vanilla and roses.

She glanced up at him with a sad little sigh. "Oh, Gabe. If any man could tempt me now, that man would be you."

He pressed his lips to her hair. "How 'bout this, then? Could you be with me for right now? You're not going anywhere for months, right? There's plenty of time for us to just be together. We could see where it goes between us. All I would ask is that you try to keep an open mind and heart."

"It seems so dangerous…"

"Most good things involve an element of risk."

She chuckled. It was the sweetest sound. "Gabriel Abernathy, you are far too convincing, you know that?" They stared at each other.

He dared to suggest, "So, that's a yes?"

When she didn't say no, he saw his chance

and lowered his mouth to hers. She didn't pull away.

He gathered her closer, grateful for this, at least—the feel of her small, soft body in his arms again at last, for her kiss that was sweet and tender, with a promise of more.

He lifted his head sooner than he wanted to, just to show her he understood the meaning of restraint. "Yes?" he asked again.

Her eyes were deep as oceans. "What do you do to me?"

He smoothed an errant lock of hair away from that irresistible mouth of hers. "Everything. I hope. If you'll let me."

She put a hand to his chest. He wrapped his fingers around it. "Okay. We'll, um, try again." And she dipped her head a little shyly. "Whatever that means."

He tipped up her chin so she was looking in his eyes again. "How about we start with right now and the whole afternoon and on into the evening?"

She laughed and playfully pushed him away. "You're not wasting any time."

"Hell, no."

"It is nice here." She lay back on the blanket, laced her fingers behind her head and stared up at the shifting leaves of the cottonwood overhead. "So the plan is to just hang out by the creek, you mean?"

He thought of Gramps and the other information he'd uncovered yesterday. She'd just agreed to give him another chance. He almost wanted to forget the diary and the sad story it contained.

But she'd asked to meet Gramps. And for a moment, Gramps had blasted through the wall of his own silence. He'd commanded Gabe to bring her to Snowy Mountain. There seemed no choice now but to go forward, to do what he could to solve the old mystery. "Well, there is something else I've been meaning to talk to you about…"

She'd shifted her gaze from the leaves above to his face. "What's going on?"

He stretched out beside her, bracing up on an elbow so he could look down at her and hold her gaze. "I've been out to see

Gramps twice since our night together—last Friday and then again yesterday afternoon. I really have been thinking about the story of Josiah and Winona and the missing baby Beatrix."

"Did something…happen?"

"Not on Friday. I told him about the diary that day, and a little about you. He didn't respond. I got nothing, you know? It's the way he is most times now, like the lights are on, but nobody's home."

She reached up and laid her hand on the side of his face. "I'm sorry. I know how much you love him. It must be so hard."

He caught her fingers and kissed the tips of them. "Yeah—but anyway, then you called on Saturday and I was a jerk. After that, I couldn't stop thinking about you, about what an idiot I am and about Gramps, too, and the story of the diary. So I went to see him again. I talked about you and the diary. He was silent. I got nothing. But then I got up to go and he spoke. Just a few words. He said, 'Bring her to me.'"

A small gasp escaped her. "He meant me?"

"Yeah. He meant you." Gabe almost told her the rest of it.

Don't give up on love, Gramps had commanded.

But no. The way Gabe saw it, at this point those words were just for him. She wasn't ready to hear them yet.

She sat up. "Does that mean you're taking me to meet him?"

He nodded. "If you still *want* to meet him."

"Oh, Gabe. Yes. I do."

"There's more…"

Her eyes widened. "Tell me."

"All right. I started thinking of ways to find out if the Abernathys of Rust Creek Falls might have anything to do with my family. At lunch yesterday, I asked my dad and my grandfather about the family history in Bronco and about my great-great-grandparents, Gramps's mother and father. My dad and Grandpa Alexander weren't very helpful. They both insisted that the

Abernathys have 'always' lived in Bronco. Grandpa Alexander didn't remember a lot about Josiah's parents, except that they were kind of distant and strict. Later, it occurred to me that property sales are a matter of public record. And if my family showed up here seventy-plus years ago and bought the ranch that is now our Ambling A, there would have been a deed, proof of the sale and when it happened."

"You mean, at the county offices somewhere?"

"Well, as it turns out, I didn't have to look that far. My grandfather has the information in the safe in the office at the main house. He's very proud of the fact that it's a fireproof safe, impervious to burglars and whatever. Also, he assures me the deed is duly recorded at the assessor's office."

"So then, when did your family acquire the Ambling A here in Bronco?"

"In 1920, my great-great-great-grand-father, a wealthy speculator from back east, bought up several parcels from poor farmers who'd gone bust after claiming the land in the land run a few years earlier."

"Wait. So then, you're saying your family has owned the ranch here in Bronco since 1920? Are you trying to say that proves they *aren't* the Abernathys who vanished from Rust Creek Falls?"

"No."

She sat up and slapped him playfully on the arm. "Gabe. What are you getting at?"

He sat up, too. "My family has owned the land for a hundred years. But they didn't incorporate it into the Ambling A until seventy-five years ago. My great-great-grandfather, Josiah Sr., did that."

Her sweet mouth dropped open. "That would have been about the time the Abernathys in Rust Creek Falls disappeared."

He grinned. "It doesn't really prove anything."

"I know. But it does kind of give me the shivers."

"Yeah. I have to admit, I got a shiver

or two myself when I saw that the dates match up."

"So then, you told your grandfather about the diary?"

"I didn't need to. As an Abernathy heir, I'm expected to take an interest in the ranch and everything else my family owns and/or controls. I also have the combination to the safe. My grandfather Alexander didn't question me when I said I wanted to look over the articles of incorporation."

"I think what you're telling me is that you didn't explain to your grandfather about the diary because you were afraid that if you shared the real reason for your interest, you might upset him. Is that right?"

"Pretty much. You saw how *I* reacted when you told me—and really, didn't we just agree that nothing is in any way proven yet?"

"Fine. I get it. Until we have a better idea of what really happened in the past and if your family might be somehow involved, why take the chance of getting everyone stirred up?"

"Yeah. I'm thinking that at this point the story of the diary ought to be on a need-to-know basis."

She was frowning. But then she nodded. "Okay, that makes sense—yet you did tell Josiah."

"Because he might be the key. Somewhere deep down, he might know everything. As for my dad and my grandfather, though, I really do think they're completely in the dark about what happened seventy-plus years ago. I'm not ready to go there yet with them."

"Yet. Meaning you will in the future?"

"Meaning, let's talk to Gramps first and then take it from there."

She was tugging on that loose thread in the blanket again. "I feel a little guilty. I confess, I can't make myself ask Winona if she might be the woman in the diary."

He stilled her hand. "It's done, Mel. I

talked to Gramps about the old story. He said to bring you to see him."

"You're braver than I am."

"Naw. But I *am* curious. Very curious. So? You up for meeting my Gramps today?"

Mel wanted to pick up the diary on the way to Snowy Mountain West. That worked for Gabe. He needed to have a look at the old book and the letter, anyway.

He followed her to her place, where Homer greeted them at the door. The kitten jumped on Gabe's boot and started chewing on it. "Hey, buddy. Easy there…" He picked up the little guy and Homer instantly began to purr. "I think he really likes me."

"No doubt about it." Mel dropped her keys on the entry table, crossed the room to the bed and took a worn, leather-bound volume from the bedside drawer.

Gabe set the kitten down and Homer darted away. With the diary pressed against her chest and apprehension in her eyes, Mel returned to where Gabe stood at the door.

"Do I get to see it?" he asked when she stopped in front of him. She nodded and held it out. He took it. "Bejeweled, no less."

"Fancy, huh?"

He traced the tooled letter *A* centered on the cover. Different-colored stones encircled it. He opened the book to the first page.

"Is the handwriting familiar?" she asked.

"No. But I don't recall ever really noticing Gramps's handwriting."

"Maybe if we could get a sample of something he wrote, we could take it and the diary to a handwriting expert." She gazed up at him through hopeful eyes, her soft cheeks pink with excitement.

"Maybe."

Her expression turned rueful. "I guess I shouldn't go getting ahead of myself here, huh?"

She looked so sweet and sincere. He wanted to drop the old diary on the table next to the keys she'd put there and pull her into his arms. They could spend the day in her bed instead of trying to coax information from an old man who rarely spoke anymore.

Could she read his thoughts in his eyes? It sure seemed like it. "Oh, Gabe," she whispered. "I keep saying I'm leaving at the end of the year, that I don't want to get anything started with you, but this past week, I couldn't stop thinking about you. Even though I was mad at you, I really did miss you. So much."

He set the book down by the keys, after all, and eased a hand around the silky nape of her neck beneath the glorious tumble of her long, blond hair. "And I missed *you*— everything about you. From the sound of your laugh to that sharp tongue you've got. And then there are those unforgettable blue eyes." He brushed his thumb across her cheek. "And this naughty dimple right here. I missed this dimple so damn much."

The dimple in question deepened with her radiant smile. "Yeah?"

"No doubt about it." How could he resist?

He swooped in and claimed that gorgeous mouth.

She swayed closer and he wrapped her up tight in his arms, her scent of flowers and sweet vanilla making his head spin and his blood run hot in his veins. The kiss kind of took on a life of its own. She opened to him and he swept his tongue into the wet heat beyond her parted lips. He could have stood there, kissing her endlessly, into the next decade and beyond.

But finally, she pulled back a fraction and drew in a slow breath. "Okay. Enough of your amazing, distracting kisses, Gabe Abernathy. We're on a mission today. I want to meet your great-grandfather. Please?"

Regretfully, he set her away from him and picked up the diary. "All right."

She hesitated. "I didn't show you the letter. Do you want to read that first?"

"Later. Right now, let's just go." She picked up her keys. He caught her hand. "You're riding with me."

Did he expect the usual pushback? Yep.

But he was pleasantly surprised when she said, "Fair enough. But I do need one of these keys to lock the door."

"I'll allow that." With a finger, he eased a heavy lock of hair behind her ear. And then he couldn't resist bending closer, brushing his lips across hers just one more time.

She made the sweetest, softest little sound of pleasure, like a moan that got caught on a sigh—and then she pressed her hand with the keys in it against his chest. "We can't stand here all day, kissing at the front door."

He brushed his mouth across hers a second time. "Oh, no?"

She gave another sweet sigh—and then pushed against his chest a little harder. "Out the door, mister. Now."

Gabe felt a rising sense of anticipation as he ushered Mel into the reception area at Snowy Mountain West.

"This is nice." She gave him one of those glowing smiles of hers. "It's open and inviting."

"Snowy Mountain is the best around. Especially for memory care. The environment is secure and comfortable with open rooms and wide hallways that are easy to get around in. Residents are monitored round-the-clock. Staff-to-patient ratio is excellent, too."

"Hi, Gabe." Linda gave him a wave from behind the front desk. She glanced down at the big laptop screen on the desk. "Let's see…ah. Josiah has just finished his supervised afternoon walk. He'll be in his room."

"Great." Gabe turned to Mel. "I just want to go see how he's doing first, before I introduce you." He gestured at a sofa and chairs near a picture window. "Have a seat. I'll come right back for you."

"Sure." Mel exchanged smiles with Linda and took one of the chairs.

Gabe found Gramps in his rooms, as promised, sitting quietly in his recliner. "Hey." He bent close. "How are you doing today, Gramps?"

As usual, Gramps gave no response. His

shirttail had come out of his belt on one side and his collar was slightly askew.

Gabe gently tucked in the loose section of shirt and tugged the collar straight. "There. You look great. And today, you're about to meet the woman you asked me to bring to you—you remember, don't you? Her name is Mel Driscoll and she's *the one*, Gramps. But remember, she's not ready for love yet. So don't tell her that I know she's the one for me." Gabe dared to look into those hazel eyes then.

Nothing. He saw nothing at all.

And that hurt. It hurt like hell every single time he had to face anew that the man who'd taught him how to *be* a man was never really coming back. Gabe would gladly offer up his big house and the fortune he'd made for himself in the past decade just to have his Gramps grin and give him a wink the way he used to do.

"Don't move," Gabe said with forced cheer. "I'll be right back."

As he retraced his steps to the welcome

area, he wondered if he was doing the right thing. What if the sight of the diary upset the old man? Now and then, Gramps did get agitated. He would shout nonsense, even throw things. Gabe would have to call the staff to settle him down. Gramps had never hurt anyone physically, but it always broke Gabe's heart to see the calmest, kindest man he'd ever known lose control.

Mel had the diary. She held it close to her body, same as she had back at her apartment, as she rose and came toward him. When she got to him, she gazed up at him searchingly. "You look...unsure. Did something happen?"

"No. It's a day like any other day. He's in his room, staring into space. You really shouldn't get your hopes up that you'll find out much from him."

"I understand."

No, she didn't. But she would soon enough. "Okay, then. This way..."

Gramps was right where Gabe had left

him, sitting motionless in his favorite chair, his eyes blank and staring.

"Gramps, this is the woman I told you about yesterday. This is Mel."

After no response from Josiah, Mel said, "I'm so pleased to get to meet you, Mr.—"

"Call him Josiah."

"Um. Josiah, then. Hi, Josiah." She gave the expressionless old man her prettiest smile, after which she sat where Gabe indicated, on the love seat across from Gramps. Gabe sat beside her. She held out the diary and started to say something, but then set it down on the coffee table and turned to Gabe. "I'm not sure how to begin..."

He doubted it would matter what she said. But she was here now, and they were set on a course. There was nothing else to do but proceed. "I already told him the basic story you told me. He didn't respond. You never know, though. Maybe if *you* tell him, the story will get through."

"Yes. All right." She launched into a brief version of the ill-fated love affair between Winona Cobbs and the young man with the same name as Gramps. "Winona had a baby," she said, holding out the diary again, explaining that the whole story was inside, including a letter tucked in the binding, written by Josiah Abernathy, who was also the author of the diary itself. "The letter says the lost baby didn't die, after all, but was somehow taken by Josiah's parents and given up for adoption. The letter claims Josiah knew who the adoptive parents were. Josiah, would you like to see the letter?"

Gramps didn't answer. He didn't even move. His eyes seemed focused on nothing and everything at once.

Mel shot a worried glance in Gabe's direction.

What could he say? "Sorry. I don't think he's going to be responding today." He reached across the distance between the love seat and the recliner and clasped Gramps's shoulder. His old bones seemed to poke right through his skin. "Okay, Gramps. Maybe some other day?" Gabe started to stand.

Mel's light fingers brushed the back of his hand. "Let's stay. Just for a little while."

"He's not going to suddenly have anything to say." Irritation gave his tone a cold edge. He was angry at his own foolishness to have brought her here, made her a witness to a helpless old man's painfully diminished capacity for even the simplest sort of human interaction.

Her smile was as sad as it was angelic. "I get it. But we're here. It seems rude to just get up and run out." That cute dimple in her cheek kind of winked at him. "Sometimes, when I go to see Winona, I have a tall glass of water or a cup of tea and we just sit, you know, not saying a word, nice and quiet, enjoying the moment of being there. Together."

This woman. She drove him a little bit crazy, what with wanting her so much and trying not to lose hope that she would ever be his. She also bugged the crap out of him now and then. In addition, she kind of amazed him. Not a lot of women would want to hang around for any longer than necessary with an old man who rarely spoke and stared blankly at nothing for hours on end.

Gabe couldn't help but grin. "You want a tall glass of water, is that what you're saying?"

"Water would be perfect, Gabe. Thank you."

The room had a tiny rudimentary kitchen area—a bit of counter, a sink, cabinets containing plastic glasses and plates, a drawer with some flatware. There was also a mini fridge with an ice maker in the dinky freezer area. Gabe took down three glasses, dropped some ice cubes in each and filled them with water.

He carried them back to the sitting area and deposited them on the coffee table.

Mel pushed one over in front of Josiah and one in front of Gabe's seat. The third, she sipped from. "Thank you, Gabe. Very refreshing."

He wanted to grab her and kiss her for

being so sweet about this, for wanting to sit and visit with an old man whose visiting days were behind him. "You're welcome." He dropped down beside her and drank from his own glass.

Mel relaxed against the cushions and glanced around. Her gaze landed on a large wedding portrait on the wall by the window, behind Gramps's chair.

"That's Gramps and Great-Grandma Cora on their wedding day," Gabe said. Gramps wore a baggy suit with enormous lapels. His bride wore a forties-style satin dress with a long, white veil.

Mel frowned a little. "They look so serious."

They did, as a matter of fact. "Great-Grandma Cora was a quiet woman," he said. "It was hard sometimes to know what she was thinking. She made the best buttermilk biscuits, though. I've never tasted any to compare. And she played the piano. Holidays, we'd gather 'round, including all my uncles and aunts and cousins. Great-

Grandma would play Christmas carols and we'd all join in singing."

"My mom played the piano." Mel's eyes shone bright. "She was talented, a natural musician. I thought, since my mom had a talent for music, that of course, I would play, too."

"Do you?"

She laughed. The sound was sweet and kind of goofy, too. It tugged on a tender place down inside him. "Nope." She popped the *p*. "Frankly, I suck at it. I mean, we are talking no musical talent whatsoever."

He grinned at her. When he glanced across the coffee table, it seemed to him that Gramps had settled more comfortably into his big chair. He still stared into nowhere, his plastic glass of ice water untouched in front of him, but he seemed more relaxed about it, somehow.

The strange little visit continued in the same vein. Mel noted personal items around Gramps's room and Gabe explained their significance. She talked more about her mom and dad. It was so obvious she'd loved them very much and the loss of them remained fresh and painful for her.

Gramps didn't say a single word. He never made eye contact with Mel or with Gabe. But somehow, it felt like he was there with them, enjoying a nice visit, a little small talk and a cool drink.

If Gabe hadn't already been in love with the woman sitting next to him, he would have fallen right then, on that sunny Monday afternoon in his great-grandfather's quiet living room at Snowy Mountain Senior Care. She was not only sharp and smart and strong. Mel had a good heart, a deep and natural kindness that made her even more beautiful than her pretty face and curvy little body.

They ended up staying for over an hour. When they got up to leave, Josiah had yet to respond to their presence in any way beyond seeming to relax slightly in his chair. He sat silent, his arms stretched out, resting on the chair arms.

As Mel rose, she took the diary in one hand. With the other, she reached across the coffee table to give the back of Gramps's hand a quick, fond touch. "I'm so pleased to have met you, Josiah."

It happened right then. Gramps blinked two times and turned his hand over, palm up. His bony fingers closed around Mel's. Gabe saw it happen and heard Mel's tiny gasp. He felt a burst of pure joy—that Gramps had responded, that he *saw* Mel, even liked her.

But then alarm jangled through him. Had Gramps frightened her?

No. Her blue gaze met Gabe's and she smiled her dazzling smile. "Do you see?"

Gabe nodded, relieved Gramps hadn't scared her, glad to see her pleasure at the old man's reaction. "I do."

Mel turned her bright glance to Josiah again.

But the moment of connection had already passed. Josiah had released her. His hand lay limp—palm still turned up, fingers curled inward like a dying leaf.

"Josiah?" Mel asked softly, with the sweetest, saddest note of fading hope. "Come back..."

But Gramps's face gave her nothing. His curled hand didn't move again.

"Love you, Gramps," said Gabe quietly, hating the resignation in his own voice. "See you soon."

Chapter Nine

A few minutes later, out in the parking lot, Gabe opened the passenger's side door for Mel and she climbed in. He went around and got up behind the wheel. They hooked their seat belts simultaneously.

And then they both sank back in their seats. Maybe it was just him, but sorrow seemed to weigh down the air around them. Gabe stared out the windshield at an empty bench beneath a pretty sugar maple several yards from the hood of his F-450.

"For a moment there I really thought he might smile at me," Mel said.

"Yeah, well. That rarely happens any-more. Sometimes he speaks, but not much and usually in kind of a flat voice."

"I'm so sorry, Gabe."

"I really do think he's still in there some-where, but most of the time I have to admit that he's just…not." Was he being overly negative? She gazed at him as though she had no idea what to say. "On the plus side, the staff here is amazing. They kind of get him going on an activity and he'll sort of carry through. But it's all as though he's on automatic pilot. Going through the mo-tions by rote."

She wrapped her hands around the diary, which she'd laid on her lap. "I guess I was foolish to think he might have all the an-swers to this old mystery, huh?"

"Not foolish. Just hopeful. And there is nothing wrong with having hope. I'm glad you came to meet him, even if it didn't play out the way you might have pictured it." And there he went, being a downer again. "Look at it this way, Mel. He did seem at ease around you. You were good with him. And hey, it could be worse. I'm grateful for every minute I get with him. I visit him at least once a week and we talk—well, *I* talk and sometimes I really do get the feeling that he understands everything I say."

She shut her eyes and turned away.

"Hey, hey. What'd I do wrong now?"

Slowly, she turned to face him again, her eyes open now. Her smooth throat worked as she nervously swallowed. "Nothing, Gabe. You did nothing wrong. On the contrary. I'm just feeling a little humbled right now, that's all."

"Humbled? Why?"

"You, Gabe. Sometimes we get crossways, I know. But you are a good man. You've got a lot of heart. And wherever things end up with you and me, well, I'm glad I went trespassing on Ambling A land that first day we met."

It was far from the declaration of undying love he wanted from her, but for now, he would take it. He leaned across the wide console and ran a finger down the velvet skin of her cheek. Sweet color bloomed in the wake of his touch. "It's your night off. Share it with me. Come out to the ranch. Give my mom a thrill and have dinner at the main house. Then we'll go back to my place, just the two of us."

She tried to back out. "I don't know. I'm not exactly dressed for dinner with the parents."

"Weak excuse, Mel. It's a working cattle ranch and it's just dinner. Malone will cook and that means the food will be great. But it's not like we dress up for dinner every night. You're welcome just as you are." When he pulled her closer, she let him, and he took heart from that. "I don't want to let you go." His lips just barely brushed hers. "Not yet. Indulge me."

"I feel the same," she confessed in a whisper.

He kissed her, a slow kiss that gradually deepened. When she sighed in surrender, he wished they were anywhere but here, in broad daylight in the parking lot of Snowy Mountain Senior Care.

"Say you'll have dinner out at the ranch," he commanded gruffly against her parted lips, fully expecting more objections.

But she surprised him—in a very good way. "Yes."

He pushed his luck. "Yes, what, exactly?"

She gave a low, sweet laugh. "Yes, Gabe. I would love to come to dinner tonight at the Ambling A."

Dinner at the main house went pretty much as Gabe expected.

Malone outdid himself with his famous standing rib roast and Yukon Gold potatoes. Gabe and his dad argued over just about every subject that came up. Alexander made pronouncements concerning how nothing in the world went the way it ought to go anymore and everyone under fifty was spoiled and self-centered, unwilling to work hard to achieve their dreams.

Gabe's mom had a whole lot of questions

for Mel, all of them geared toward pinning Mel down as a prospective daughter-in-law. Gabe had to cut in when she started talking about her favorite wedding venues.

"Mom. Nobody at this table is planning a wedding," Gabe reminded her, mentally adding *yet*.

His mom waved him off with a flick of her hand. "It's idle conversation, Gabriel. Relax. I was just wondering what Mel thought of an outdoor wedding. They can really be something glorious if done right— don't you agree, Mel?"

Mel took his mother's shameless match-making in stride. "I do, yes. We've had several weddings in the town park up in Rust Creek Falls. Everybody in town is always invited. Sometimes things do get a little crazy after dark, though."

Gabe remembered the story Mel had told him the day she adopted Homer. "Yeah, some old moonshiner spiked the wedding punch once. Things got pretty wild."

His mother looked vaguely concerned.

She suddenly had other ideas. "Maybe a barn wedding. Or one at the Association. They really put on the most gorgeous weddings there. So elegant. Just unforgettable. I'm hoping I can have the Association do Erica's wedding, though she's always vague and distant about it whenever I suggest that maybe it's time for her and Peter to set a date—Peter's her longtime steady boyfriend. He's also the company attorney for his family's business, Barron Enterprises, and Erica works for the company, too. I hope she's not planning to be married there in Colorado. I mean, Montana is her home and she ought to be married here."

"It'll all work out, Mom, don't worry," said Gabe, though he had no idea whether things with Erica would "work out" or not. He just didn't want to get down in the weeds over his absent sister tonight.

"Well, I do worry," his mom insisted. "She should come home more often."

"Yes, she should," his father agreed, rather sternly. Husband and wife shared a speaking glance. Whatever Gabe's dad communicated to Angela in that look, she let the subject of Erica drop.

Once they'd finished the meal, they all went out back to sit on the patio in comfy lounge chairs. They watched the sunset and enjoyed Malone's irresistible lava cake, with brandy-laced coffee.

It was almost nine, still not quite dark yet, when Gabe took Mel back to his place. Butch, who always tagged along when Gabe went back and forth to the main house, trailed after them.

"I should go," she said as he ushered her in the front door and Butch edged around them and kept on going toward the living area. When they'd walked over to the main house earlier, she'd left her purse and the diary on the credenza right there in the front hall.

Before she could grab them up, Gabe captured her hand and pulled her close. He wrapped both arms around her. She felt so right pressed tightly against him. "Stay."

"Oh, Gabe…" Her body said yes—but he could hear the doubt in her tone, see caution in her eyes.

He caught a lock of her hair and smoothed it over her shoulder. "Life's too short. But still, you keep running away. Stay. Just for a little while."

The thing was, Mel wanted to stay. So much. She wanted to spend the night in Gabe's bed.

She wanted it to be more than a rebound with him. She truly did. Every moment she spent with him, she liked him more. *Trusted* him more.

And that made her afraid she was only setting herself up to be hurt again.

"If you hurt me, Gabe…" She let the words trail off without finishing her thought, let her wary expression speak for her.

He framed her face between his warm, rough palms. His eyes burned into hers, begging her to believe. "Not gonna hurt you, Mel."

"I don't *want* to trust you, but then somehow I can't help myself." She pressed a hand to his hard chest. "I'm starting to believe you, Gabe. Starting to think that you are actually for real."

He put his hand over hers, pressing her palm more firmly to his chest. Beneath the layers of muscle and bone, she felt the strong, steady rhythm of his heartbeat. "This is special, you and me," he said. "I'm not messing with you. Yeah, I've never gotten close to forever with anyone before. And I get that people think that's a bad sign, that a guy needs to be practicing commitment from an early age or he's not a good risk when it comes to love. Sometimes people are wrong. Sometimes a guy is just waiting for the right woman to come along."

Her breathing had gone a little ragged and her chest felt tight. "What are you saying to me, Gabe?"

"You really want to know? You want me to say it out loud right now?"

Why was her pulse racing? She gulped, hard. "I don't think I'm ready."

And there it was, his slow, delicious smile, the one that made him almost impossible to resist. "You should get ready."

"I'm not sure I know how."

He lifted her captured hand from his chest and brought it to his lips. She felt his warm breath on her skin and prayed that, whatever this was with him, she wouldn't blow it and neither would he. That they would ultimately be bigger than their fears and their doubts, that neither of them would end up letting the other one down.

And she thought of the diary waiting a few feet away, of Wren Crawford, of the crazy idea the little girl had that the diary brought love to whoever possessed it. She saw herself, not long from now, passing it on.

Passing love to the next person.

After claiming it for herself.

"It's all right." Gabe pressed those wonderful lips of his to the back of her hand and a thrill vibrated so sweetly down the length of her spine. "It's gonna be all right." He said it as a promise, a solemn vow.

Her doubts reared up again. "How can you know that, Gabe? How can you be sure?"

"I know one thing." Oh, those eyes of his. So steady, sky-blue. And true. That was the thing about Gabe. She was honestly beginning to believe that he would know what Todd Spurlock hadn't—how to be true.

"What one thing do you know, Gabe? Tell me, please."

He gazed at her for a long time, his eyes holding hers, before he said softly, "No. Not tonight."

She groaned. "You're a tease, Gabe Abernathy."

"Yeah, probably. But you did say you're not ready."

He was right, of course. She might have begun to wonder if there really was something kind of magical about the diary, but she wasn't ready to hear any brave declarations. Not right now. Not tonight.

He bent close to nuzzle her neck. She let out a low moan as he scraped his teeth down the side of her throat, leaving a hungry trail of sparks in his wake.

"Stay with me tonight." He breathed the gruff words into the tender crook of her shoulder.

She could feel him growing hard against her belly. And that hot shiver running down her spine? It was spreading out inside her, turning slow and lazy like warm honey, touching her everywhere, making her tremble in her boots.

She stretched her neck back, giving him better access. He scattered sweet kisses along the side of her throat. "Well, the more I think about it, the less I want to leave right now." Her voice sounded slow and lazy, hungry and very willing to her own ears.

"Stay as long as you want, Mel." He scraped his teeth along the line of her jaw and nipped playfully at her chin. "Stay forever."

She started to tell him that she really

wasn't ready for forever. But before the words took form, his mouth claimed hers. She drank in the taste of him. Their tongues were dancing.

Dancing, yes…

He danced her backward, kissing her as they went—across the entry hall, through the big, open living room with its enormous fireplace, down a wide hallway and into the master suite.

Standing by the huge bed, he undressed her, pressing kisses on the bare skin he revealed as he peeled her clothes away. "You are perfection, Mel. This shoulder…" He kissed the outer curve, where her shoulder met her arm, as he dropped her shirt to the rug. His lips traced a path to the base of her neck and then across her collarbones. "Perfection."

She closed her eyes on a heavy sigh, every inch of her open, willing, deliciously aroused, as he took her bra away and lavished kisses on her bare breasts. She threaded her clutching fingers into his hair, trying to hold him there.

But he was on the move, trailing those lips of his down the center of her body.

Blinking like a sleeper half-awakened from the deepest dream, she stared down at him as he dropped to his knees before her. He was looking up, his eyes waiting. Their gazes met and held.

He took her hand and braced it on his broad shoulder. She held onto him for balance as he lifted her right foot and took her boot away. He peeled off her thin sock and then repeated the process with her left boot.

A moment later, he was pulling down her jeans, taking her little pink thong with them as he went. When her jeans and underwear got down to her ankles, she stepped out of them and lightly kicked them aside. It seemed surprising in that moment that she was totally naked and he still had on all his clothes.

Not that she cared who was naked, who wasn't. He had her completely at his mercy.

She was needy and yearning, ready to be his.

And he made her more ready with those clever, stroking hands of his, with that mouth that knew magic spells to cast on her. That mouth was everywhere, taking control of all her most secret places. She welcomed him, opened to him willingly, and she cried out his name over and over as she came.

The second time he took her over the edge of the world, as she was still quaking at the sheer beauty of the things he did to her willing flesh, he lifted her up and set her on the bed. Her body felt heavy and hungry, ablaze with desire. A quivering mess of pure sensation, she fell back, arms and legs limp. Staring up at him through dazed eyes, she watched as he swiftly and ruthlessly stripped away his own clothes.

He was magnificent, looming above her, his body lean and cut, a racehorse of a man, beautifully masculine, his eyes holding hers, not letting go as he took a condom from the bedside drawer. She reached for him with a cry of need and pleasure. He came down to her, wrapping her up in his heat and his strength.

They rolled together, holding on so tight, kissing so deeply, their bodies on fire. He was ruining her; she knew it. After this, after Gabe, there would never be another man who could possibly compare.

No, she wasn't ready for him. Not ready for the promise of the diary, either. Not ready for any of this, really. She'd had all the right plans once, known just where she was going and how she would get there.

But her perfect plans had come to nothing.

And now she was here, with Gabe. And in this moment, right now, her failure to judge the true character of the man who'd betrayed her didn't matter. None of that mattered, really—all her careful machinations to make the right choices, to engineer a good life with a trustworthy man who'd turned out in the end to be anything but.

Some things, a girl could never be ready for. Some things, a girl just had to give herself up to and hope that happy-ever-after was more than some romantic fool's impossible dream, more than a promise of love in a tattered, bejeweled, leather-bound journal found hidden in a run-down ranch house three hundred miles away—a promise destined to be broken in the most tragic way.

Gabe rose up above her, his eyes blue fire now. She watched him roll on the condom.

She begged, "Please, Gabe. Please, now..."

And then he was there, all around her, holding her, in her, *with* her in the truest way.

True. He was true—in his heart. As a man. And she believed in him.

At least in that moment, she believed. She believed she had everything—Gabe in her arms and hope in her heart.

Her body rose to the crest again. She whispered his name that time, holding on tight as her climax rocked through her. And then she pulled him even closer. He was lost to his own pleasure, moving hard and deep within her. She held him, loving the desperate way he groaned her name as he came.

Mel hadn't meant to fall asleep in Gabe's giant bed with its frame and four posters made of massive, rough-hewn logs.

But every time she started thinking she needed to get up and go, he would pull her close and cover her eager mouth with his—and the heat between them would rise again. Sometime after 2:00 a.m., the night must have caught up with her. She'd closed her eyes, just for a moment...

And when she opened them, daylight was peeking through the blinds.

She sat up and shoved the tangled mess of her hair out of her eyes. It fell right back down again. She blew at it, accomplishing nothing, and finally raked her fingers back through it, until it stayed off her face. "I need to get going."

Gabe didn't answer. She glanced down at him to see if he was still asleep. That was when he reached out, wrapped a hand around her arm and pulled her down on top of him. "In a little bit." He tried to kiss her.

"Hey!" She shoved at his beautifully muscled bare chest. "I mean it. I have to go."

"No, you don't."

She glared down at him, though it was hard to be crabby when he looked so rumpled and sexy, his hair spikier than ever, a sleep mark on his beard-scruffy cheek. "Homer chews on my things when I'm gone too long. I really hope he didn't find a way to get into my closet."

"That cat needs a trainer." He tried to pull her close again.

She fake punched his rock-hard shoulder. "Stop right there, mister. Or you're getting a big dose of morning breath."

"Give it to me, baby. Give it to me now." He pursed his lips at her and scrunched his eyes shut.

She laughed and squirmed away—and then couldn't resist wriggling close once more. He banded an arm around her. For a moment, they just lay there, with her tucked nice and cozy against his side. She could have stayed like that forever, wrapped in the tangled sheets, the two of them, Gabe and Mel.

It felt so right. It felt like this, with Gabe, was how it was really supposed to be, that maybe her whole life had blown up in her face because it was the *wrong* life all along. And the wrong life had brought her to the threshold of the right one.

Sheesh.

She really needed to put a lid on all these romantic fantasies she found herself indulging in lately.

One day at a time, Mel. Yeah, Gabe was a great guy, but that was no reason to go fantasizing about forever.

He dropped a quick kiss on the top of her head. "Coffee?"

She put her silly, romantic musings away and grinned up at him from the cradle of his arm. "I thought you'd never ask."

He tipped up her chin and kissed the tip

of her nose. "You got it. I'll go make some." He rolled from the bed, so gorgeous, so naked. She could have lain there staring at him for hours. But then he grabbed yesterday's jeans and yanked them on.

She sat up and blew her sleep-mangled hair back out of her eyes again. "Is it okay if I use the bathroom, freshen up a little?"

"Go for it. I'll look into rustling us up some eggs."

Gabe had the coffeemaker going and was about to grab the eggs from the fridge when his dad spoke from behind him. "Still got company this mornin', I see."

Wincing, Gabe shut the fridge door and turned to face his father, who held the diary in one hand and Mel's purse in the other. "You know it's rude to just bust in without knocking, Dad."

"And you oughta start locking the damn front door."

"I never felt I had to—until right this minute, anyway."

His dad shrugged. "Relax. Your mom and I just happened to notice that you never drove Mel home last night."

"What are you telling me? You two lurked out on the front porch, listening for the sound of my pickup driving away?"

"What can I tell you, son? We're not getting any younger and neither are you. I see the way you look at Mel. I think that girl's special to you and I also think it's about damn time. Can you blame your mother and me for being anxious? Your mom longs for grandkids. Your sister is a lost cause. Even if she married that guy in Denver and they had some kids at last, she would likely never bring our grandbabies home to us. It's your job to give us some babies to spoil."

"You are so far out of line, Dad. This is so wrong."

"See now, I think it's a fine thing for me and your mother to make our wishes known. I like that girl. It's more than clear that *you* like that girl. And it's about time you settled down. You can make an honest woman out of her and make your mother happy, too."

The thing about George Abernathy was he thought he knew everything. And even when Gabe wanted what his dad wanted, somehow Gabe felt all wrong about agreeing with George—and more so than ever right now, when it came to Mel.

Mel was skittish about this thing between them. The last thing she needed was to walk in on his dad with his big mouth, going on about how he approved of her as a prospective daughter-in-law while simultaneously implying she'd be something of a slut if she didn't get Gabe's ring on her finger immediately.

"How many ways can I say this? Stay out of it, Dad."

His dad didn't even blink. "That coffee smells good. I'll have a cup." He set Mel's purse on the breakfast table and held up the diary. "What's this?"

Gabe had no intention of going into all that right now. "It's not yours. Put it down."

"It's old, isn't it? And it's got a big *A* on the cover."

"Thank you, Captain Obvious," he muttered under his breath.

"I heard that. Smart-ass." George flipped back the front cover. "What the hell?"

"Put it down."

"Josiah Abernathy?" He pointed at the first page. "This has Gramps's name in it. And the Ambling A...in Rust Creek Falls?" George's eyes, the same pale blue as his own, accused him. "What's this all about? Are you trying to tell me this is Gramps's old diary from way back in the day?"

"Dad. I'm not telling you anything. Put it down."

George poked a finger at the first page. "Why in hell would Gramps keep a diary? And why does it give a Rust Creek Falls address for the Ambling A? This doesn't make a damn bit of sense to me."

"Good morning, George." Mel, fully dressed, with her hair falling just so and her face freshly scrubbed, stood in the open arch that led back to the master suite. Damn, she was something. It had to be awkward for her, to find his dad in his kitchen after spending the night in his bed.

But Mel didn't seem bothered. She exuded calm confidence.

Gabe's dad glanced up from the old book he should never have touched and smiled— a warm smile. He did seem pleased to see her. "There she is. Pretty as a picture. Good to see you again, Mel." He brandished the diary some more. "Found this in the front hall, along with your purse."

"Ah. Yes, well…" Mel drew in a slow breath and sent a quick glance at Gabe. Her eyes asked, *What now?*

He gave her a slight shrug.

Really, what could they do at this point but explain the situation? It would most likely all come out in the end, anyway, whether Gramps and the brokenhearted boy who'd written the diary were one and the same, or not.

Mel read his expression as though he'd spoken aloud.

At her slight nod of acceptance, he turned to his father. "Okay, Dad."

George peered at him sideways. "Okay, what, exactly?"

"Sit down, have some coffee. Want some eggs?"

"I could eat." George shot a glance at Mel and then swung his narrowed eyes back to Gabe again. "What's going on?"

"Here's what. I'll pour your coffee and scramble the eggs. Then Mel will tell you a story…"

Chapter Ten

A half an hour later, when Mel finished sharing the story contained in the diary, their coffee cups were empty. Their eggs sat untouched. Mel didn't much like the tense expression on George Abernathy's face. He looked a little pale, too, especially around the mouth.

The big, beautifully rustic kitchen was deadly quiet. Butch, stretched out on the floor by his water bowl, scratched at his ear. The tags on his collar clattered together, the sound shockingly loud in the too-silent room.

Finally, George picked up the diary, which he'd set on the empty chair next to him. He waved it at her. "You're saying all that you just told me is in here?"

"Yes—except for the part about how Beatrix survived and was adopted by some other family, a family never named. That part is in a letter Josiah wrote to 'W,' whose name was actually Winona, at the psychiatric facility she was sent to in Kalispell, a letter he never mailed."

"Where is this letter?"

"In the diary."

George flipped the diary over and ruffled the pages. Nothing fell out. "Where?"

She held out her hand. "I'll be happy to show you." His expression wary, his eyes guarded, George passed her the diary. She folded the front and back covers open until they touched and carefully pulled the flattened, folded envelope from its slot in the binding.

George snatched the envelope from her hand. "Give me the diary, too."

She felt suddenly, ridiculously possessive. She wanted to clutch the old volume to her heart and never let it go—which was beyond ironic. From the first, she'd tried to deny the diary's hold on her. She'd been telling herself it had nothing to do with her, that it wasn't her story, that the old book had been dumped in her lap and all she wanted was an excuse to get rid of it.

Well, George Abernathy, who watched her, narrow-eyed, his mouth a thin line, was offering her exactly what she'd been so sure she wanted, the perfect excuse to walk away.

And yet here she sat, longing with all her heart to hold on, to never let go until she'd found Winona's daughter and reunited her with the frail old woman in Rust Creek Falls—and with Josiah, too.

Because who did she think she was kidding, anyway? She did believe. She believed that Gabe's dear old Gramps had written the diary and that *her* beloved Winona was the missing Beatrix's rightful mother.

Gabe seemed to understand how she felt—her feeling of ownership, that she wasn't finished yet with her part in this. "Dad," he said gently, "the diary doesn't belong to you."

George huffed in outrage. "It's got my grandfather's name in it written in my grandfather's hand."

Mel's heart stopped dead in her chest—and then began racing. "How do you know that?"

"I know Gramps's handwriting like I know my own."

Gabe shook his head. "Oh, come on, Dad. You're exaggerating."

George huffed out a hard breath, glanced away, and then back. Gruffly, he backpedaled. "Well, I'm pretty sure, anyway."

"Dad." Gabe's voice was gentle. "Slow down. Mel's the one who was given the diary. She's in charge of this situation and I'm helping her in any way I can. She and I are dealing with this. You can't just jump in and take over."

"Have you already tried to talk to Gramps about it?"

"We did. We told him everything Mel just told you. But you know how he is nowadays."

George looked so sad suddenly. "Nonresponsive?"

"That's right. But we're still on it, Dad. I promise you we won't stop until we've figured out who's really who and exactly what happened."

We? Did Mel like the sound of that too much? Was she getting in way too deep here?

She did. And she was.

George's beefy shoulders slumped a little. "Well. Ahem." Suddenly, he didn't look so proud and imperious. For the first time in Mel's limited experience with the man, it appeared that George Abernathy might defer to his only son. "At least, I would like to be kept in the loop. I want to know whatever you find out."

Gabe glanced at Mel. She realized he was

waiting for her answer. "Yes, of course," she agreed.

"There's more," the older man said. "I would like to feel free to share what you've told me with Angela and my father and others in the family. I see no reason that the events chronicled in that diary should be kept a secret."

"You're right," Mel admitted. "Gabe and I agreed to keep the story to ourselves until we knew more. We thought that there was no reason to get everyone excited when we're still not absolutely positive that your Gramps and the author of the diary are one and the same."

"That story shocked the hell out of me, I admit." George pushed his untouched food aside and rested his forearms on the table. "My immediate response was denial. But the more I think about it, the more I realize I don't know that much about my great-grandparents, really. And neither does my father." George turned to Gabe. "As your grandpa Alexander told you the other day at lunch, he found your great-great-grand-father Josiah and your great-great-grand-mother Noreen cold and judgmental and impossible to get to know. As for Gramps, he never said much about them, either. There are holes in our family history. And they kind of line up with the events in the diary. I can't tell you much of anything that happened in the family before Gramps married Cora—which reminds me, Gabriel. Your grandfather told me that you'd been asking about the deed to the Ambling A."

"That's right. I was trying to find out what I could about how the family came to Bronco. I still don't know anything for sure about that."

"Son, the truth is, none of us do. Except maybe Gramps—and he's all locked up now inside his own mind. What we do know is that the ranch didn't formally become the Ambling A until seventy-five years ago. I'm guessing that would be right about the time what's described in the diary took place?"

Mel confirmed that. "Yes, it would."

"So, there we are." George looked ten years older, somehow, than he had when Mel first entered the kitchen and found him standing there with the diary in his hand.

"Nothing is proven," Gabe reminded him.

"Maybe not. But I feel the truth of it down in my bones."

"Okay then. You are now in on this, Dad. You know what we're trying to find out and we can use all the help and information we can get. The best way to do that is to ask anyone who might possibly know something about the past."

"Works for me," said Mel.

"I'm in," said George.

"With one stipulation," added Gabe. "We all agree that information sharing goes both ways. We need to be working together on this. You share whatever you find out," he said to his dad. "Mel and I will do the same."

"Like I said, I'm in," George solemnly replied. He held up the letter to Mel. "I would like to read this now."

"Yes. Please do."

The old paper crackled as George removed the single sheet from the wrinkled envelope and scanned the few lines it contained, after which he carefully refolded the letter, put it back in the envelope and handed it to Mel. She returned it to its place in the diary's binding.

George asked, "Has anyone checked with the hospital in Kalispell where Winona Cobbs was sent?"

Regretfully, Mel shook her head. "Wilder Crawford, whose family now owns the Rust Creek Falls Ambling A, told me that the hospital burned down forty years ago. Back then, all the records would have been on paper, so that's kind of a dead end. Not to mention, if we could find somebody who knew something, they would be in their nineties, at least, and no doubt reluctant to share patient information due to confidentiality laws."

"Well, that's discouraging." George picked up his coffee mug, started to sip from it, realized it was empty and set it back down. "I have another request, Mel. I would appreciate a chance to read the diary for myself."

Again, Mel felt that strange reluctance to part with it. But in the end, she knew she would have to accept that the old journal was never meant to be hers to keep forever. "Gabe hasn't read it, either," she said, glancing at the man in question. "I'll leave it with him."

Gabe said to his dad, "Once I've read it, I'll give it to you with the understanding that it comes back to me—and then back to Mel—within a day or two." An unwelcome shiver went through Mel as he said that. She was getting the feeling that her time with the old book was ending. She should be happy about that. She'd never wanted it in the first place. But she didn't feel happy. She felt angry and sad and very confused.

"All right, then." George picked up his coffee mug and pushed back his chair. "We're in agreement. I need more coffee. Anybody else?"

A half hour later, George had returned to the main house and Gabe stood at the fancy chef-style range scrambling more eggs to replace the ones they hadn't felt like eating while Mel related the story contained in the diary.

Mel sat at the table, sipping another cup of coffee, her eyes drawn to the man at the stove. His broad, muscled back was to her. He still hadn't put on a shirt and his feet were bare. He looked amazing from behind and right now, he reminded her of the lonesome cowboy she'd believed him to be the first day they met.

Warmth pooled in her midsection and she heard herself sigh as she watched him spoon the eggs onto the plates and pop the toast from the toaster. He was spreading on the butter, the knife scraping across the toasted bread, when the terrifying realization hit her like a bullet straight to the heart.

He turned with a plate in each hand.

I'm in love with this man.

The words took form in her mind and she recognized the absolute truth in them—at the same time as she knew with total certainty that she couldn't go there.

She simply could not. Not now. Not…for the longest time. Maybe never. She wasn't ready.

Not for this. Not for love.

She'd known Gabe for less than three weeks. Just a month ago, she was about to marry Cheating Todd. She'd thought she'd loved *him* at the time. She couldn't just turn right around and fall for the gorgeous man who stood above her now. She was smarter than that.

He set one of the plates in front of her. "You okay?"

"Uh, what? Yeah. Sure. Fine."

"You don't look fine. You look like you just got some really bad news."

"No. Uh-uh." She pasted on a big smile. "It's nothing." And she was such a big, fat liar.

He bent close, brushed her lips with his. Longing speared through her—for everything. A lifetime. True happiness. Forever love.

With *him*.

Oh, dear God. What was the matter with her?

It was one thing to lose her head while he was making her moan his name in bed— natural, really, to get swept away in the moment, to tell herself little fantasy stories about how the diary had done its work and brought her true love.

But to indulge herself in thoughts of love now, the morning after?

Uh-uh. Not good. Not possible. No way.

This was so dangerous. The whole point, after the abject awfulness of her breakup with Todd, was to make an independent life for herself, to find happiness on her own terms, not defined by a man.

Not even *this* man—who was as beautiful inside as out.

The whole point was to have *no* man. To be complete and content, self-sufficient financially and emotionally, all on her own.

"Hey, now," he said softly. "Hey…" He set down his plate, too. Then he took her hand and pulled her out of the chair. She went, feeling numb. Disembodied.

Except for her heart. Her heart yearned. Her heart…loved. Her heart felt like it was trying to batter its way out of her chest to get closer to him.

Even though that was impossible. Even though she could not be in love with anyone right now.

Gabe wrapped those hard arms around her. For a moment, she gave in, let herself lean on him. She drank in the strength of him, the warmth of him surrounding her.

She felt his lips in her hair. "Tell me," he whispered. "What's wrong? Talk to me."

"Listen, I…" She made herself look up at him and then had no idea at all what to say.

Gabe tipped her chin up with a gentle touch. "You're scared. Of what?"

"I…think I feel too much for you."

He gazed at her for the longest time. "Let me be sure of what you're saying. You feel strongly for me and that scares you?"

"Yeah." Her voice was small. Weak to her own ears. She made herself speak with more force. "After Todd messed me over, I promised myself I would find my way, on my own. I promised myself I would make my life—a good, full life—without a man in it. And then you came along and I'm, well, I'm getting ideas, Gabe. About you. And me. Together. In a permanent way."

His smile was slow and oh, so tender. "I would like that. A lot. More than anything else in this world. It's what I want, Mel. You and me. Together. In a permanent way. Mel, I'm in lo—"

"No!" She pressed her fingertips to his lips. "I can't hear that now."

He wrapped his hand around hers and

kissed the fingers that had shushed him. "I don't get it. Why not just hear me out?"

"Because I'm weak. I want to believe you and I can't afford to do that." She searched his face. "I'm sorry, I really am, that we're not on the same page about this. My heart tells me to trust you."

"So listen to your heart." His voice was low, carefully controlled, but charged with strong emotion.

"Gabe. I can't. I have to do what's right for me. I just wish you could understand that."

He dragged in a slow breath. "I'm trying. And I do get it. I hate it, but I get it. Take your time. Think it over."

"Oh, Gabe. I don't know how I'll think of anything else."

He stroked her hair. "You want to run away, don't you? To hide from this, from you and me?"

"Yeah. I do. A little."

He chuckled. It wasn't a happy sound. "More than a little, I think."

"I just, well, the last thing I expected was you."

"Well, you got me. And I guess I'd better not say more until you're ready to hear it." He took her by the shoulders. "Tell you what."

She caught her lower lip between her teeth. "Hmm?"

"We've already thrown out one batch of perfectly good eggs. Let's eat these before they get cold, too."

She gave him a slow nod. "Yeah. Good idea."

So they sat down and had breakfast. A silent breakfast, during which she couldn't help feeling she was throwing away the best thing—the most important thing. At the same time, she felt bound and determined to carry through with the promise she'd made to herself, to create a life on her own.

They cleared the table and loaded the dishwasher. By the time that was done, the silence between them felt like an open wound.

Had she done that? Wounded him?

He said, "I get the feeling you're leaving now."

"Yeah. I think I'd better go. I need to get in to work early. The boss is coming into town to see how I'm doing." She'd been looking forward to catching up with DJ Traub. He was a good guy and a great boss.

"Right." Gabe picked up the diary from where she'd left it, on the table. "I was watching your face when my dad asked to read this. You seemed uncomfortable with the idea of leaving it here."

How did he know her so well? "I was. I am. I've grown kind of attached to it. But I know that I need to let go. You need to read it and I think your dad does, too."

"You're sure?"

Dear Lord, he was the most beautiful man. She wanted to grab him and hold him, to drown in his sweet kisses. To never, ever lose him.

And yet, here she was, walking away.

Was getting a little distance from him the right thing to do now—or simply proof of her fear he would break her heart if she gave him too much power over her?

She answered his question about the diary. "I'm sure. I want you to keep it."

"All right." His fine mouth was a bleak line. "I'll get it back to you in a few days."

"No!" The word escaped her of its own volition. She sounded panicked. With considerable effort, she softened her tone. "I mean, really. After you and your dad read it, your grandfather will want to read it, too. And your mother. And what about your dad's brothers? And your cousins? I think a whole bunch of Abernathys are going to want to know about Josiah and Winona. They'll want to try to figure out where Beatrix might be. I'm starting to accept that my part in this old mystery is pretty much finished. Through some crazy twist of fate, I brought the diary to Bronco—to you and your family—where it needs to be. I think it's time for me to let it go. I'm turning the search for the truth over to you."

Something had happened in his eyes. They were no longer warm as a summer sky, but wintry. Cold. "It's one thing to turn your back on me, Mel." His voice chilled her.

She gasped. "But I'm not!" It was a lie. After today, she fully intended to stay away from him, to give herself some much-needed distance from the danger he posed to her vulnerable heart.

And he knew it, too. "You're walking away from me, Mel. And you're a liar to say you're not. I don't like it, but I get it. I know you're scared, though I am not that SOB in Bozeman."

"I don't think that you're like Todd."

"Yeah, well. Could have fooled me. And hey, I understand your fear that I might just do you like he did. I'm willing to wait, back off, give you the time you need to see how wrong you are. What I'm not willing to do is watch you drop this diary on me and walk away. You're in this and you need to stay in it. You're the connection to that woman named Winona in Rust Creek Falls. Are you just going to turn your back on her, too?"

"Of course not."

Those ice-blue eyes said he didn't believe her. "You're lying to yourself as well as to me. That woman believes her child died being born. What if Beatrix is still alive today? What if there's a chance your Winona could be reunited with her daughter? You're just going to walk away from that, dump it all in my lap? What if your help would make the difference, somehow? Gramps and Winona are both in their nineties. They don't have a lot of time."

"I'm aware of that."

"Then what are you doing? What if your walking away slows the whole process down just enough that Winona doesn't live to meet her own daughter?"

"That's crazy. That's not going to happen."

"You don't know what could happen— what *will* happen. Stop kidding yourself. What about that guy named Wilder whose family lives in the house that more than likely once belonged to my great-great-grandparents? What if I need to talk to that guy? Are you going to make me do that without you?"

She drew herself up. "Wilder will be glad to talk to you. You don't need me for that."

He shook his head slowly. "You just won't admit what you're doing, will you?"

She couldn't bear to tell him the truth— so she lied some more. "I don't even know what you're talking about."

He held up the diary, held it right in her face. "This—what's in this old book here— it's a sacred trust and you damn well know it. You didn't want to take it on, but you knew that you *had* to take it on. Why are you suddenly ready to just drop it and run?"

"Gabe, I... Look, I didn't just drop it on you."

"Yeah, you did. You know you did—and

no, Mel. You don't get to dump the diary on me and walk out the door to your independent life where no one can ever hurt you again. Not without me first telling you exactly what I think of what you're doing."

Her throat felt tight. She ordered her lungs to draw in a slow, shaky breath. "You're not being fair."

"You're right. I'm not. I don't want to lose you and so I'm not playing fair. I'm not keeping my mouth shut while you walk away and tell yourself you somehow did the right thing by turning your back on me and Winona and Gramps and a missing little baby who never knew who she really was."

"You're way overreacting." She tried to stay reasonable, to keep her voice even and calm.

"Wrong. The truth is, I was *under*reacting. I was trying hard to be understanding. I was going to let you walk out on me without a fight in hopes that you'd realize on your own what a mistake you were making and finally come back to me. But, Mel, you went too far. You dumped the diary on me and said you didn't want it back. You did that for one reason and one reason only— to cut ties with me completely."

Panic rattled through her. She had done exactly that—and now she couldn't stop herself from jumping straight to denial. "No. No, that's not—"

"True? Yeah, it is. You're willing to abandon the truth in order that you won't have to talk to me or have me reach out to you." He shook his head slowly. "I gotta tell you, Mel. I'm not very *understanding* about that. I'm not letting you go without telling you what I think of what you're doing. I damn well am being honest, Mel. And you? You're lying to yourself and acting like a coward, to boot."

She was shaking. She couldn't take any more. "I can't do this. I need to go."

For several truly awful seconds, she was certain he would light into her again. But then he only scooped up her purse from the chair at his side and shoved at her. She took it from him as he muttered, "Fine. Let's go."

With trembling fingers, she hooked the strap on her shoulder. "Listen. Whatever you need from me, concerning anything in the diary—anybody in Rust Creek Falls you need to get in touch with—of course, I'll help in any way I can. You just have to call and I'm on it."

He only stared at her, his cold eyes giving her nothing. Finally, he shrugged. "I'm not calling you. You want out, you're out. Come on, I'll drive you home."

The ride to Bronco Heights seemed to take forever. Mel stared blindly out the windshield most of the way. Neither of them said a word.

When he pulled to a stop in front of BH247, she didn't know what to say to him. She had this ache in her chest and she had a really bad feeling it was only going to get worse. If she'd imagined she could leave this man and be untouched by what she'd had with him, however briefly…

Well, she'd been deluding herself.

Her stomach churned. Her heart ached with desperate yearning—for the chance she couldn't make herself take, for what she was throwing away. This really was the end for them and, well, she had this sudden awareness that she'd made a whopper of a mistake in calling it off between them.

And now it was too late. He really seemed done with her in a very final way.

And his being done with her was only what she'd asked of him.

It hurt so bad, much more than she'd allowed herself to admit that it might—and she had only herself and her fearful heart to blame.

All it took was one quick glance at his steely expression and the hard set to his jaw to know there was nothing she could say right now to make this moment better.

She unlatched her seat belt. "Thanks, Gabe. For the ride. For…everything."

He turned his head and faced her then. His eyes remained that frosty blue, distant and withdrawn from her and all they might have been, if only she'd been braver, truer. Or at the very least, willing to risk her heart again. "Goodbye, Mel."

She yanked on the door latch and got out of there, fast. Eyes front, she raced for the building. If she so much as hesitated, she might just whirl and run after his big pickup as he drove away.

It took forever, or it felt like it, to get to her door, to let herself in. She shut the door behind her, dropped her purse to the floor and then let her knees give way, until she was sitting there, her back against the door, her breathing ragged and frantic, her heart pounding so hard she almost feared it would explode inside her chest.

Across the room, Homer sat on the foot of her bed. He watched her through those enormous gray-green eyes.

"Hey," she said weakly, still gulping in air.

Homer jumped down and came to her.

She held out her hand and he ducked under it. Scooping him up, she cradled him to her chest, pressing her ear against his soft fur so his welcoming purr radiated through her.

For a long time, she just sat there, holding the purring kitten. At some point, the waterworks started. She ugly cried, getting snot and tears all over poor Homer. He didn't seem to mind. He didn't even try to squirm away from her, just let her hold him and cry on him as he continued to purr.

She cried for her parents, cried for all the love they'd given her so freely, all the years of tender care. For all the love she had within her, stored up for them. They were supposed to be there, for her wedding to just the right guy, to be grandparents to her children, to be among the ones she loved and cared for as the years went by and they needed her more.

She missed them still. She always would. The loss of them remained, an empty space inside her, an empty space that echoed with all that would never be.

And what about Cheating Todd? Yeah, she cried for him, too—well, not for the reality of Todd. But for who he was supposed to be. The man she'd created in her heart, the shoes that the real Todd had never actually filled.

And Gabe?

Him, more than anything. She cried for what might have been with Gabe, for the love that she couldn't quite bear to accept from him. Because her heart just wasn't ready. Because after losing her folks and then saying yes to a man who had turned around and betrayed her, well, she just wasn't able right now to trust her own judgment. Not with something so scary and overwhelming as love. She could end up with a big hole inside herself, another terrible emptiness like the one her parents had left through no fault of their own.

Or with a deep and abiding sense of betrayal, an anger that gnawed at her, like the smoldering fury she'd been gifted with courtesy of Todd.

It was too much, what Gabe had asked of her. Too much to ask and much too soon.

She'd been right to say no to him. She would get over this pain. Even though, at this moment, it felt like her heart was breaking for the third time.

Even though now it seemed to her she'd just thrown away everything she needed most.

Chapter Eleven

After a good hour of bawling on the floor, trying to convince herself she'd done the right thing to end it with Gabe, Mel finally dragged herself to her feet and got down to the business of pulling it together enough to go to work.

Hiding the ravages of her long crying jag wasn't easy, but after sticking her face in a sink full of ice water and piling on the concealer, she hoped maybe she looked at least presentable. She arrived at DJ's Deluxe a full hour before she was expected.

DJ Traub was already there, sitting behind his giant desk in his private office in the complex of offices on the floor above the restaurant. His door was wide open, as usual.

Mel pulled her shoulders back and tried to look cheerful and confident as she tapped on the door frame to get his attention. His gaze shifted from his laptop to her at the sound.

"There's my favorite manager." He rose to greet her. "Come in, come in."

In his forties now, Dalton James Traub was a handsome man. He had that steady, boy-next-door quality that made others trust him. A family man to the core, he'd been happily married to his wife, Allaire, for as long as Mel had known him. From the day he hired her to wait tables at his Bozeman Rib Shack, Mel had admired not only DJ's genius as a successful restaurateur, but also his big heart. He was good to the people who worked for him, paying them well, offering decent benefits and reasonable hours.

He came around the desk to meet her and they shared a quick hug. When they pulled apart, she could see by his worried frown that all that concealer hadn't hidden as much as she'd hoped.

"Sit down." He gestured at the seating area over by the tall windows that looked out on the street. Reluctantly, she went over and took a chair. He shut the door and dropped onto the leather sofa across from her. "What's happened?"

She smoothed her hair and crossed her legs and tried to look breezy and relaxed. "Long story. Nothing to do with the job, DJ, I promise you."

"I've been over the books. I know we're doing just fine here—better than fine. And I've spoken with both Gwen and Damien. They have nothing but good things to say about you. You're doing a terrific job, as I knew you would. But I'm not asking about DJ's Deluxe. It's you I'm concerned for."

"I'm fine."

"I don't think so." He frowned. "How long have I known you?"

"DJ, I mean it. I'm okay."

"Just answer the question. How long?"

She glared at him for several seconds, but he didn't back off. "Eight years or so?"

"And I've only seen those haunted eyes I'm lookin' at now one other time."

Mel knew he wasn't referring to her breakup with Todd. When she'd visited his corporate offices in Bozeman last month in search of a job to tide her over until the one in Austin opened up, she'd held it together just fine. Why?

Because I was more angry than broken-hearted over what happened with Todd.

Right now, she felt shattered.

And she hadn't felt shattered since...

Her throat got tight and her lower lip started trembling. She ordered it to stop and said softly, "You mean the day I got the news about my parents..."

DJ gave a slow, solemn nod. "You don't break easy, Mel Driscoll. So when you do,

I notice. I care about what's going on with you. Tell me what the problem is. You never know. Maybe I can help."

"You're the best. But there's nothing you can—"

"Try me."

"It's a relationship thing. You don't need to listen to me whine about my love life, or lack thereof."

"Let *me* decide what I need, Mel. Talk."

She shouldn't. It was so completely unprofessional. But DJ was a good guy and he really seemed to want to help. "I, um, think—well, I've just totally blown it with a very special guy. I'm sad, really sad. I'm also disappointed in myself. I promised myself I wouldn't fall for him, but apparently, my heart failed to get the memo. Now I've broken it off with him and I feel horrible. I've ruined everything with him and there's no going back. It's over. I kind of hate myself, if you want to know the truth."

"Hating yourself will get you exactly nowhere."

"Yeah, well, hating myself may not be constructive, but I seem to be doing it anyway."

"And as far as you and that special guy being 'over,' you might be surprised. It might all work out for you two in the end, after all."

"Of course, you would say that, DJ." She'd seen him and his wife together more than once during the years she worked for him in Bozeman. "You and Allaire have been married for as long as I can remember. You're in love and have been forever and you naturally think everyone's going to end up happily married to the perfect person, too."

"Mel. You don't know the whole story. Allaire and I, we had a very rocky start."

"It couldn't have been that bad. It's obvious you two were meant for each other."

"Allaire didn't think so at first."

That made no sense. "What do you mean?"

"I mean, I always loved Allaire, but she

chose my big brother. She and Dax got married right out of high school."

Okay, that was a stunner. "You're not serious."

"As an overcooked tenderloin. My heart was broken. I knew I would never get over it."

"But it *did* work out for you and Allaire."

He nodded. "Her marriage to Dax didn't last. They were divorced within a few years. And more than a few years after that, I came back to my hometown of Thunder Canyon to open a Rib Shack at the resort there. I tried to stay away from my brother's ex-wife. But it was impossible. Within a few months, she had my ring on her finger. Allaire is the love of my life and I can't imagine my world without her in the center of it. So cheer up, Mel. Have a little faith that things will work out just right in the end for you and that special guy."

She longed to believe him. But she didn't. "I'm leaving in January. You know that, DJ. My perfect job is in Austin."

"It's just a job, Mel. And maybe your guy will decide he wants to move to Austin, too."

"Uh-uh. I mean it. He and I are over."

DJ just wouldn't give it up. "We'll see. And there's another possibility we haven't discussed yet..."

She braced her elbows on her knees and propped her face in her hands. "What are you getting at?"

"You know I think you're the greatest. I like to work with the best and the brightest and that means I'm not happy with the idea of losing you again when you head off to Austin at the end of the year. I've been plotting a way to keep you right here in Montana where we both know you belong."

"I'm not staying in Montan—"

"Hold on, now. Let me finish. I've always wanted to boot myself in my own ass for letting you go when you moved over to Spurlock's. I've followed your career, Mel. I know you're a brilliant finance and insurance manager. And I believe you really ought to aim higher."

Cautiously, she prompted, "Higher, how?"

"Would you consider becoming CFO for DJ's, Incorporated? You could work out of the offices here—yeah, you would have to travel to the main offices once or twice a month, but it's not that far and your home base would be Bronco if you want it that way."

She felt suddenly breathless. "CFO for DJ's, corporate…"

"That's right. Our current CFO is retiring. He could work with you starting next month, until you both felt you were ready to take over the job from him. Think about it. Think of what terms and salary and options you would want, what kind of benefits package. Think of how you would see your role as Chief Financial Officer for our restaurants and how you would grow the role. If you're interested, we'll work up an offer and take it from there."

"DJ, I think my head is spinning."

"I can understand that. It's a lot to consider, especially on the heels of what just happened with your special guy. My plan was to be here in Bronco until Friday, but I can stay till Saturday. You can take a break to think things over and I'll cover for you."

"A break? You mean extra time off?"

"Just an extra day or two."

"That's not necessary."

"I say it is and I'm the boss. We should spend some time today going over everything. I want a report from you on our systems and on the front and the back of the house. Just a general rundown on how we're doing at DJ's Deluxe and what could be done better. Then there's the dinner service. We should both be there for that, so I can check on how it's going, and we can consider solutions to any issues that crop up— all of which means I'll need you for the rest of the afternoon and tonight. But I don't want to see you here tomorrow, Thursday or Friday."

"DJ, that's thoughtful of you. But I really don't need two extra days off."

He put up a hand to silence her. "At least take tomorrow. And then Thursday is your regular day off. That will give you two days to clear your head a little, figure out what you want for your future, get closer to a decision about your next step. And, Mel, I sincerely hope that your plans for the future will include working out whatever's wrong with your guy and joining the DJ's team on a permanent basis."

Twice that evening, Gabe realized he couldn't stand *not* to make things up with Mel. Both times, he grabbed his keys and went out the front door, jumped in his pickup and kicked up a cloud of dust heading straight for town and DJ's Deluxe. The first time, he stopped himself at the Ambling A's front gate. The second time, he made it halfway to Bronco before he forced himself to pull over and turn the damn truck around.

Mel was done with him. And he was through with her. He needed to accept that—get over her and move on.

The second time he made himself return to the ranch, he locked himself in the house and got out the whiskey. He would get good and drunk, drown his sorrows at the loss of the gorgeous little blonde with the smart mouth and the naughty dimple in her soft cheek.

But then he only had one drink—a double—and put the bottle away. Because getting blasted wouldn't end his misery. It would only give him a hangover tomorrow, make him more miserable than he already was.

He took a shower and went to bed—with the diary. It wasn't his first choice for a bedmate, but Mel was not available. And she wasn't going to *be* available. He needed to accept that, get used to it, move on.

The diary would have to do. He stayed up all night reading the damn thing, poring over each page, studying the brief letter hidden in the binding. The experience really fit his mood that night. Just what he needed, a sad story of thwarted young love and a lost child, a child yet to be found, seventy-plus years later.

Was the Josiah who wrote the diary really his own Gramps? He couldn't be sure. There was no incontrovertible proof and there might never be.

But he felt strangely certain anyway. Josiah and Gramps were the same person. And the baby named Beatrix, wherever she was now, deserved to be found.

It was after four when he finally dropped into an uneasy sleep. At a little after eight, the ringing of his cell jarred him awake.

He grabbed it off the bed table and glared at it before taking the call. "Erica. What?"

"Good morning to you, too, Mr. Crabby Pants."

"It's 8:00 a.m. and you sound way too cheerful."

"I like to get up and get going on the day.

You, on the other hand, sound like you were up all night doing things you shouldn't."

He thought of Mel. Gone. He wanted her back. It was going to be damn hard not to jump in his truck and drive like a bat out of hell straight to BH247 in the next hour or so. And then later, not to just happen to drop in at DJ's Deluxe to see if maybe there was a chance she'd rethought walking out on him and couldn't live without him, after all.

Damn. He was hopeless. He needed to grow a pair and forget her.

"Gabe? You still with me?"

"Right here. Everything okay?"

"Um. Fine. Just checking in, you know?"

Did she sound a little off? "What's happened, Erica? What's wrong?"

"Not a thing."

"You sure?"

"Of course."

"How's the boyfriend?"

A beat of silence, then, "Peter's fine."

"Something's up. Talk to me."

"Stop it. There's nothing. I just called to say hi."

"Let me guess. You're coming home for a long visit."

Another silence. That meant she wasn't. "Soon, I promise."

He wanted to ask why she never kept her promises—not the ones about coming home, anyway—but that would only start a fight and he really didn't want to fight with her. "We miss you. Gramps isn't doing well and you need to—"

She cut him off. "Can you just not get on me about Gramps, please?"

He opened his mouth to insist that she needed to be here, that Gramps needed to see her.

But who did he think he was kidding? These days, Gramps seemed so far away from everyone, trapped in his own head, never really seeming to know the difference between Gabe and any random, helpful Snowy Mountain caregiver.

"Okay," he said. "Sorry. Love you, little sister." And he did—but he had resentments toward her, too. She'd drifted so far away from the family. He worried about her. Sometimes he wondered if everything in her life really was as perfect as she kept insisting it was.

And he didn't know how to talk to her. He wanted to tell her about Mel—loving her, losing her—and the diary and the possibility that their beloved Gramps had a lot of secrets he'd never shared with the family.

But then she said, too cheerfully, "And I love you. How is everything there?"

He played the dutiful big brother and reported that everyone was fine, that Grandpa Alexander could never figure out why young people thought they knew it all and Dad refused even to consider a single one of the suggestions Gabe had for streamlining a few things around the Ambling A. "And you know Mom. She's waiting for the go-ahead to start planning your wedding."

Erica muttered something under her breath.

"What? Didn't catch that."

"Oh, nothing," she answered airily, eva-sive as ever.

And when she said goodbye a few min-utes later, he heard the line go dead and felt more disconnected from his sister than ever.

The next day—her extra day off, thanks to DJ, who refused to believe that she would prefer to keep busy—Mel knew she would go nuts if she hung around her apartment. She was up at seven and the day seemed to stretch out in front of her, empty and endless. She knew she would only end up knocking on her neighbors' door, inter-rupting Amanda's workday, crying on her shoulder and then imposing her misery on Brittany, too, when she got home.

No. Mel couldn't bear a whole day of dragging around the complex, playing the sad sack, taking advantage of her new friends' affection and goodwill to moan about how she and Gabe weren't working out. Especially given that she was the dumper and not the dumpee.

She needed action. And she really wanted to get the heck out of Bronco, where everything reminded her of Gabe.

She decided to visit Winona. The long drive to Rust Creek Falls would clear her head—she hoped. Also, she ought to check on the various repairs at her parents' house. The new tenants were moving in on the first and the place had to be ready for them.

Homer could go with her. It would be good for him to travel a little, start becoming accustomed to being in the car.

Once she was packed and ready to hit the road, she decided she ought to give her friends a heads-up. Brittany and Amanda would worry if she simply vanished for a couple of days—and strangely enough, the thought of how concerned they would be lightened her spirits a little. She might have blown it with Gabe, but she *had* made two true friends during her weeks in Bronco.

Amanda answered the door at Mel's

knock. In shorts and a tank top, she had her hair piled up in a messy bun. "Hey, Mel."

Mel recognized her friend's distracted expression. "You're working."

"You know me. I'm *always* working. Come on in."

"No, I won't keep you. I just wanted you to know I got two days off in a row and I'm driving up to Rust Creek Falls. I've got a friend I need to check on and some other stuff I really have to take care of."

Amanda's smooth brow crinkled. "Everything okay?"

"You know how it goes. There's always something."

"You want to talk?"

Mel kept her smile in place. "Thanks, but it's a long drive. I need to get on the road."

After another searching look, Amanda let it go. "So you'll be back…?"

"By Friday. I have to work Friday night."

"Homer?"

"He's coming with. He doesn't care much

for car rides, but I'm hoping he'll get used to it."

"I'll be glad to kitty sit."

"Thanks, but I kind of like his company."

"Okay, then. See you Friday. I'll tell Brittany." Amanda held out her arms. They shared a quick hug and Mel found herself thinking that no matter where she ended up at the first of the year, she would be keeping in touch with Amanda and Brittany.

Homer did create something of a challenge. She strapped his kitty carrier in the back seat, and he began wailing in misery the second she started up the car.

Mel drove straight to the pet store and bought a giant tube-shaped cat cage big enough for several toys, a treat dispenser and a soft-sided, collapsible portable cat box. She spent a while introducing him to his new travel space and teaching him how to get his treats, petting him constantly and reminding him what a very good boy he was. And then, once they got back on the road, she stopped every half hour to pet him some more and shower him with praise.

All the stops added more than an hour to the trip, but the extra space, restroom accommodations, treats, toys and attention worked. By the time they reached Great Falls, Homer had stopped crying. She continued to pull over and check on him hourly after that. And he seemed perfectly content in his giant cat tube. He even purred when she praised him.

She arrived at the house in Rust Creek Falls at five thirty and got right to work, bringing in her small suitcase and setting Homer up with his bed, litter box, play structure and food and water bowls. She raided the shed in back where she'd stored her rollaway bed, basic kitchen stuff, towels and toilet paper.

At six thirty, she strolled over to Crawford's General Store to pick up the minimum in food items—eggs, milk, bread, a few condiments, some cheese and lunch meat. The girl behind the counter there was someone she didn't recognize. That made her sad. Always in her memory, members of the Crawford family would be there to greet her any time she shopped at their store.

Back at the house, she ate a sandwich, petted her kitten and inspected the premises. The new paint looked great, the leaky pipe under the kitchen sink had been replaced and the hanging light fixture in the dining area no longer blinked on and off when she flicked the switch. Everything was ready for the next family to move in.

Now what? Her plan was to give Winona a call in the morning. She could just as easily try her now...

But she didn't feel up to dealing with anyone—not even Winona—tonight.

Alone. Brokenhearted. Antisocial. And lonely.

It was not her finest hour.

She ended up, phone in hand, sitting on the rollaway in the empty bedroom that had been hers growing up. As she petted

Homer, who was curled in her lap, she wondered what Gabe might be doing. Her longing to call him was so strong it hurt.

Somehow, she kept herself from doing that.

Finally, around nine, she went to bed. Her sleep was fitful. She woke before dawn thinking that it really was time to let go of this house. The happy memories she'd collected here would always be hers to keep. But now it was time to let some other family call it their own.

"Once the new tenants' lease is up, I'm selling this house," she informed Homer as she dished him up some Fancy Feast. Then she sat back on her heels and watched him chow down, waiting for the feeling of panic to rise as it had every other time she'd seriously considered putting the house on the market.

There was no panic. Only a sense of quiet acceptance.

After breakfast, she called Winona, who took four rings to answer and sounded a bit distracted at first. "Mellie? Is that you? What's going on?"

"I'm here, Winona, in Rust Creek Falls. I drove up from Bronco yesterday. I was wondering if I could come over and visit you?"

"Right now? Why, that would be wonderful! I'll get the kettle going."

Mel put Homer in his small carrier and took him along.

Winona was standing in her open doorway when Mel started up the front walk. She looked so thin, fragile as old glass, the network of wrinkles on her face etched deeper than ever. But her smile made the day brighter. She reached out her thin arms and Mel went into them. "Mellie, it's so good to see you." Winona took her by the shoulders and beamed at her some more. "Come in, come in!" She stepped aside so Mel could enter, glancing down at the pet carrier as Mel went by. "What is that you've got—a pet?"

"Someone very special." In the living

room, she set the carrier on the floor and unzipped the flap at the top.

Homer popped his head out of the opening. "Reow?"

Winona laughed in delight. "Look at those eyes!"

Mel scooped him up and held him close. He purred against her chest. "His name is Homer."

Winona clapped her hands. "He is definitely a Homer. Perfect choice for a name—oh!" She pressed a hand to her chest. And she was panting.

"Winona?" Mel let Homer wriggle to the floor and jumped up. "Are you—"

"Fine, dear. I am fine." Carefully, her hand still on her heart, Winona lowered herself to the sofa. "There." She drew a slow breath and then another. "Better."

"Let me call your doctor for you."

"No. There's no need. I am fine."

"Winona, you don't seem fine."

"It was just a little breathlessness. It's passed now." Winona positioned a pillow against the armrest and started to lie down. But then the teakettle whistled in the other room and she popped back up again.

"Rest," Mel commanded. "I'll deal with the tea."

"I don't mind—"

"Lie down, Winona."

With a sigh, Winona kicked off her shoes and stretched out.

"How about the afghan?"

"No, thank you. I don't need it. I'll just rest for a moment." The kettle continued to shriek from the other room. Winona gave Mel a too-sweet smile. "See to the kettle, dear."

"I will." Mel spoke sternly. "Do not get up."

"I won't."

"I'll be right back."

In Winona's little kitchen, Mel spooned Darjeeling into a tea ball and put the ball in Winona's old Blue Willow teapot. She poured the hot water over it, covered the pot with a hand-crocheted cozy and left it to steep for a few minutes.

Back in the living room, she found Winona asleep. Homer had jumped up on the sofa with her and was curled in a ball at her side. Mel bent over her. She seemed to be breathing normally.

"Don't fuss." Winona's eyes popped open. "I told you. I am fine."

Mel straightened. "I just don't feel right about you living here all alone."

Winona petted the kitten, who purred his approval. "But of course, I'm not alone. I get an endless parade of visitors checking on me daily."

"What visitors?"

"One of the Crawfords is always coming by, and usually a Dalton or two." The Daltons—and the Crawfords, who owned the general store—were well-known local families. Winona scratched Homer's ears. "And this little guy's namesake comes to see me, too. Homer Gilmore drops by two or three times a week. He's just fine, Homer is, in case you were wondering. Still living off somewhere all on his own. No one's quite sure where."

"I'm glad to hear he's doing well. Rust Creek Falls wouldn't be the same without Homer Gilmore popping up when you least expect him."

"What I'm saying, dear, is that I'm *not* alone. Someone is always showing up at my door—and what about that tea? I was thinking Darjeeling…"

"The Darjeeling is brewing."

Winona gave her a wistful little smile. "I've been longing for Darjeeling. And you picked up my mental signal. We've always had that special connection, don't you think?"

"Yes," Mel said affectionately. "We have."

Winona frowned. "If only I weren't so tired all the time."

Mel got up. "Come on, now. Lie back down."

Winona didn't even try to argue that time.

She put her head on the pillow and Mel spread the afghan over her.

The tea forgotten, Winona slept.

Mel wandered back to the kitchen and brought in the tea tray. She poured herself a cup and watched over her slumbering friend. Homer jumped onto the sofa again, cuddled up to Winona and closed his eyes.

Mel sipped her tea, her thoughts straying where she shouldn't let them go—to Gabe. How could she feel such longing for the man she'd run from just the other day?

And the diary...

She decided that when Winona woke up, she would ease into the subject of Josiah and the missing Beatrix.

But "ease in" how, exactly? She had no idea where to start.

And the more she thought about it, the more she feared the shock of the news might have Winona breathless and panting again—or worse.

Really, not much had changed since the last time Mel had visited her friend. Winona was delicate. Startling news might have a devastating effect on her.

No. Mel just wasn't ready to chance sending Winona over the emotional edge. At the very least, Mel needed to find out what had happened to Beatrix before delivering upsetting information to an old woman in questionable health.

But she wouldn't be finding out anything, now would she? She'd turned her back on the diary, left it—and Gabe—behind.

Carefully, she set her empty teacup on the tray. Guilt and shame twisted in her stomach. Gabe had been right. She'd dumped the diary on him and run away—because she was afraid. Of his love.

Of risking her heart again.

The tea had grown cold when Winona opened her eyes and sat up. Homer jumped from the sofa and darted around the room, batting at shadows.

"Oh, my dear," said Winona. "How rude of me, dropping off like that."

"I'm glad to see you resting."

"You are the sweetest girl." Winona frowned at the teapot.

"It's gone cold, I'm afraid. I'll make some more."

"Would you? I would love a cup. Old Gene brought me a red-velvet Bundt cake with cream cheese frosting yesterday." Gene Strickland ran the local boarding house with his wife, Melba. "It's in the upper cupboard on the left. Why don't you cut us each a slice?"

Mel made more tea and served it with the cake. It was after eleven when she put Homer back in his carrier and left Winona's little house.

"Be safe and well and happy," Winona whispered in her ear as they shared a last hug at the door.

Mel walked back to her parents' house, waving at former neighbors along the way, worried for Winona, yet feeling a little less glum to see some familiar faces.

But then she turned the corner and saw

the Jaguar parked at the curb in front of the house.

Clutching Homer's carrier tighter, Mel picked up the pace. A few seconds later, she spotted Todd, perfectly pulled together as usual in Western-cut dress slacks, a crisp white shirt, a butter-soft suede jacket and a pair of high-dollar boots. He was standing on the front porch, waiting for her.

"God, you are beautiful," he said as she climbed the porch steps. His perfect white teeth flashed with his too-wide smile. "I've missed you so much, Mel. You'll never know." He started to reach for her.

She jerked back as Homer hissed in his carrier.

Todd winced. "What's that? A cat? You've got a cat now?"

"Yes, I do, Todd. Why are you here?"

He raked his sleek brown hair back with a manicured hand. "You won't talk to me. I've called, I've texted. I'm at the end of my rope over you. Mel, I cannot live without you." He dropped to a knee and put his hand on his heart. "Won't you please come back home where you belong?"

She couldn't suppress a snort of laughter. "Todd, wake up. I fell for your lies twice. But then you cheated in our bed and I caught you in the act."

"No! I never cheated—I mean, except that one time."

"Stop. You did. You know you did—and so do I. And besides, one time was more than enough."

"But you have to believe me. It *was* one time—the *only* time…" He tried to grab her free hand. She jerked it out of the way. He sneezed and Homer let out an angry yowl. "Can you put that cat over there?" He pointed to the far end of the porch. "You know I'm allergic."

"Get up off the porch floor and go home, Todd."

"Mel, come on. It was a mistake and I swear on my undying love for you that it was the *only* time."

"Yeah, right. What about that earring I found under the bed a year ago?"

He widened his eyes in a failed attempt to look totally innocent. "It was yours."

"It didn't belong to me and we both know it didn't. And what about that woman, Brandi, the one with the enormous breasts who kept sexting you? You swore it was a wrong number. But it wasn't. Was it, Todd?"

"Why won't you believe me? I was wrong to cheat, I get that." Todd jumped to his feet then. "But I never lied to you. I love *you*, Mel. I've *always* loved you."

"I want you to leave, Todd." She spoke slowly and carefully, as though to a stubborn child. "I want you to go now. If you don't, I'm calling the sheriff's office. In Rust Creek Falls they don't take kindly to trespassers like you."

From the carrier, Homer let out a long, low growl. It was a sound Mel had never heard the kitten make before. She almost grinned. Her little Homer had a protective streak.

"That cat is a menace," muttered Todd.

Simultaneously, a rusty voice from somewhere near the bottom of the steps said, "Git, you durn fool! The lady asked you to leave."

Mel turned toward the voice just as Homer Gilmore rose from the boxwood bushes her mom had planted fifteen years before. "Homer?"

"'Lo, Mellie Driscoll." Homer wore his usual tattered bib overalls and a torn thermal shirt. What remained of his hair had bits of leaves stuck in it. And he had that thoroughly Homeresque expression on his hangdog face—kind of a cross between utterly benign and capable of unimaginable acts of mayhem.

"This is a surprise," Mel said fondly.

"Who the hell is that?" Todd was looking a little alarmed.

"That's Homer Gilmore," Mel replied.

"And he doesn't want you here any more than I do."

Homer mounted the steps slowly, those wild eyes of his locked on Todd. "What'd I say to you, city boy?"

"Ahem. Well. I don't—"

"Skedaddle!"

By then, Mel was having to exert a lot of effort not to burst into peals of laughter. And it got better. Todd kind of zipped around Homer and sprinted off down the steps to his gleaming car.

"You're making a big mistake, Mel!" he shouted as he flung the driver's door wide and got in.

"Git!" Homer roared again and started down the steps.

That was enough for Todd. He revved the engine and sped off down the street.

"Good riddance to bad trash," muttered Homer. "And he better slow down or he'll be spendin' the night in the county jail. Sheriff Christensen's got no patience for rich guys in fancy cars."

"Thanks, Homer." Mel reached out and gently patted the sleeve of his dingy thermal shirt.

He peered at the cat carrier. "What've you got there?"

"Homer Gilmore, meet Homer the cat."

A rumbling sound escaped the human Homer. It took Mel a moment to realize it was a laugh. "You named your cat after me?"

"I did, yes."

"Well. What do you know about that? I believe I am honored, Mellie." He peered more closely at Homer, who peered right back. "He has beautiful eyes."

"Just like yours, Homer."

The old man let out a snort. His scruffy, wrinkled cheeks had turned red. "Now you are embarrassin' me."

She patted his sleeve again. "It's almost lunchtime. Come on inside and I'll make you a sandwich."

Homer put up a gnarled hand. "Thank

you, but no. I'm on my way to see Winona. She usually has something sweet for me."

"I think it just might be red-velvet Bundt cake."

"Now, we're talkin'." He went on down the steps. At the bottom, he paused. "You take care now, Mellie Driscoll."

"You too, Homer." She gave him a wave. "You, too."

As she turned for the house, she was thinking of Gabe. Seeing Todd again had brought it all sharply home to her. Gabe was nothing like Todd. Gabe didn't have a cheating bone in his whole big, hot, broad-shouldered body.

"I really messed up," she whispered to no one in particular.

She'd been fighting it so hard, but seeing Todd again had done it, made it impossible for her to keep denying the truth.

Not only was she in love with Gabe Abernathy, she wasn't going to be happy without him at her side. Breaking it off with him had been a terrible mistake.

If only she'd figured that out before she told him they were through.

Chapter Twelve

An hour later, Mel had packed everything up, stored her rollaway and boxes of kitchen and bath stuff in the backyard shed, loaded up the car and gotten Homer all comfy in his giant tube carrier. She hit the road for Bronco.

And she made great time, too, arriving at BH247 at a little after six that evening. It didn't take long at all to bring Homer in, fill his food and water bowls and unpack her suitcase.

"Hey, neighbor!" Brittany called from the next-door patio as Mel sat out at her little cast-iron café table with her feet up on the extra chair, sipping a tall ice water and debating what to throw together for dinner. "I stopped for takeout tacos on the way home," Brittany said. "There's plenty. Join us?"

"Best offer I've had all day."

Mel went next door, where Amanda had whipped up a pitcher of margaritas to go with the tacos.

Mel offered a toast. "To you, both of you. I'm so glad you're my friends and it's good to be home." *Home.* Somehow, so quickly, Bronco had started to be the place she called home. She thought about that "dream job" in Austin. It didn't seem so perfect for her now.

"So how was Rust Creek Falls?" asked Amanda.

Mel gave a quick report of her visit and a blow-by-blow of Todd's unexpected appearance.

"Whoa," said Brittany. "I think I'm a fan of this Homer Gilmore guy."

"Me, too," agreed Amanda. She turned her big brown eyes on Mel. "I can see why you named your cat after him—and I have to ask. You seemed down yesterday. What's going on? Are you all right?"

Mel set down her margarita glass and told her friends the truth. "I'm in love with Gabe—and I broke it off with him."

Brittany looked shocked. "I don't get it. You just said you love him."

"Why break it off?" asked Amanda, bewildered.

Brittany demanded, "What did he *do*?"

Mel let out a groan. "Nothing. He was wonderful. I just got scared when he tried to tell me he loves me."

"You messed up," said Brittany.

"Tell me about it."

"You need to fix this. Go to him, tell him you were wrong and you want another chance."

"It's too late. I blew it. Falling in love wasn't in my plan and I couldn't deal with it. He's been pretty much all in with me from the first and I've been indecisive, to put it mildly, eager to be with him one minute, pulling away the next. He's through with me now and I can't blame him. I need to somehow accept that it's too late. I've blown it with him."

"Wrong attitude." Brittany shook a finger at her. "You just said you love the man. And that means it's never too late."

Amanda nodded with enthusiasm. "You have to keep trying. You have to go to him and admit you were scared, that you know you reacted badly and you want a chance to make it right."

"Tell him how you really feel," Brittany insisted. "Give your love a fighting chance."

Friday morning, Gabe got a call from Roger Dutton, a partner in his latest real estate project.

"We need to firm this deal up," said Roger. "How 'bout tonight?"

"Sure. Let's get everyone together for dinner at the Association."

"I like DJ's Deluxe," argued Roger. "Steaks you can cut with a fork, great service, good drinks and a relaxed atmosphere."

Gabe dropped into an easy chair and stared out his living room window at the mountains and the never-ending blue expanse of Montana sky. Mel would probably be working tonight.

He didn't want to see her. It would hurt like hell, having to watch her in one of those silky white shirts that clung to her pretty breasts and a black pencil skirt that made him want to bend her over the nearest available table. He didn't think he could take having to watch her fly around that restaurant, making sure everything was running like clockwork, scattering her gorgeous smiles to every man, woman and child in the place.

"Gabe? Did I lose you?"

"I'm right here."

"So what do you say? DJ's?"

No way. He couldn't do it.

And that pissed him off.

Yeah, Mel had screwed him over. But Bronco was his town. Damned if he was letting some gorgeous, unattainable blonde keep him from *anywhere* he needed to be. He would buck the hell up and deal.

Starting tonight. "All right. DJ's it is."

Someone else in Gabe's party had made the reservation, so Mel had no warning that he would be showing up at DJ's that night.

When she spotted him, he was already at his table with three other men and a good-looking middle-aged woman in a red dress. At that point, Mel was making the rounds, checking on the customers, sharing a few words at each table and then moving on.

When she stopped at Gabe's table, he didn't even look at her. Dear Lord, he was so beautiful, in a black jacket and a silver-gray shirt, his sculpted jaw freshly shaven. It was awful, knowing she loved him and having him ignore her. But she managed to keep her smile in place as she asked how everything was going.

One of the men nodded and the woman in the red dress said, "Perfect, as always. This filet is pure heaven."

"Wonderful. Enjoy your evening. And please let me know if there's anything you need." Still smiling, feeling like her face might crack, she moved on to the next table and the one after that.

As soon as she neared the hallway that led to the kitchen, she darted through it and kept going to the employee restroom in the back. It was empty, thank Heaven. She slipped in and shut the door and ended up standing at the sink, staring into her own haunted eyes in the mirror.

She needed…

"To talk to him," she whispered aloud to her own stricken reflection. "I need to talk to him. I need to be brave enough to tell him that I was wrong, and won't he please give me one more chance?" She moaned and squeezed her eyes shut. It was going to be the hardest thing she'd ever done. And he would probably say no.

But Brittany and Amanda were right. She needed to at least give her own happiness a real shot. She'd caused the breakup, ruined things between them. The least she could do was to try to fix what she'd broken.

She glared at her reflection and instructed in a hissing whisper, "You are going to do it. Tonight, if possible. And if no opportunity presents itself tonight, tomorrow you will pick up the damn phone. You will say that you were wrong and you're so very sorry and would he maybe consider—" a soft rap on the door cut her off. "I'll be right out!" she called as she flipped on the tap and washed her hands.

When she opened the door, one of the sous chefs gave her a nod and a smile and darted in as she went out.

In the busy heart of the kitchen, it was organized chaos and chef Damien reigned. He glanced up and gave her a wink and she knew that all was well in the back of the house.

Time to get out on the floor again, do her job—and watch for any opportunity to speak briefly to Gabe. Chin high and shoulders back, she headed down the hall to the dining room.

For the next hour, she kept an eye on Gabe's table. When he excused himself and made his way to the short hall that branched off the one leading to the kitchen, she shamelessly detoured to follow him at a discreet enough distance that no one would notice—she hoped.

She stood out of the way as he disappeared into the men's room. When he emerged a few minutes later, she stepped up to him just before he could escape to the dining room again.

"Gabe." She sounded like a robot—stiff. And mechanical. He looked at her as though he had no idea who she was. "I would like just a minute of your time, please."

"Why?" His wonderful face looked carved from stone.

A waiter carrying a serving tray brushed by her. She dared to touch Gabe's arm. Even through the fine fabric of his jacket, she felt him flinch—and she also felt that special energy, an arc of heat and longing between them.

Did he feel it, too? She couldn't tell. His grim expression gave her nothing.

"Over here." Did she expect him to go where she guided him?

Not really. But he surprised her and stepped back, closer to the wall, so they were out of the way. "What do you want, Melanie?"

Melanie. Well, that was a clue as to exactly how he felt about her now.

She forced herself to carry through. "Will you do one thing for me?"

"What?" His eyes were hard, unreadable.

"Meet me on the Ambling A, the spot by the creek where you found me that first day?" *Our* spot, she was thinking, but lacked the courage to say.

"Why?"

Her heart was a thousand-pound anvil inside her chest, weighing her down with regret and the sure knowledge that he was never going to give an inch. "Please, Gabe. This is neither the time nor the place. But I do want to talk to you privately. Tomorrow. Noon, at the creek. I'll be there. I hope you will, too."

"Is that all?" His voice was as cold as his icy eyes.

She was *not* going to burst into tears right here where she worked. She kept her head up and her spine straight. "Yes." And she whirled and strode blindly up the hallway to the kitchen again, so she wouldn't have to watch him turn away first.

Between that moment in the hallway and noon the next day, Mel second-guessed herself at least a hundred times. She decided there was no point in showing up at the creek—and then she decided that, even if he didn't show, she had said she would be there, and she wouldn't go back on her word. However, five minutes later, she would realize anew that there was no point in going, after all. It went on like that, her heart, her mind, her very soul seesawing back and forth between going and not going.

She hardly slept at all.

But she *was* going. She had no choice, really. She would despise herself forever if she didn't put her heart on the line for the man she loved.

Her first plan had been to bring a picnic. But last night, he'd hardly seemed in a picnic kind of mood. She would be lucky if he even showed. He was going to want to know what she had to say and very likely tell her to forget it, he was done with her.

So, then, scratch the picnic. She wouldn't even take a blanket. She would stand there on the creek bank and wait for thirty minutes. If he didn't appear, well, at least she'd shown up as she'd said she would.

She drove out to the ranch, certain she was heading for an exercise in futility and crushing disappointment.

It shocked the hell out of her to see his pickup sitting there by the road when she drove up. She pulled in behind the truck, turned off the engine, rested her forehead on the steering wheel and forced her breathing to slow to a less frantic rhythm.

Well, okay. He was here. At least she would get a chance to say what she had to say.

Her legs were shaking as she climbed the hill. At the top, she looked down, and there he was, in old jeans and a chambray shirt, facing the hill where she stood, watching her from under the brim of his dusty hat. She met his shadowed eyes, her pulse racing again, her breath sawing wildly in and out.

He was everything, all the *best* things—a cherished dream she hadn't let herself believe in. Gabe, the lonesome cowboy. Just like that first day.

Somehow, she managed to descend the

low hill with measured steps. She stopped a few feet from him. He took off his hat—because even though he didn't look happy with her, his mama had raised him right.

"Okay, I'm here," he said. "What's this about?"

She opened her mouth to tell him what was in her heart—and no words came. Her stupid lip was trembling. She bit the inside of it to make it quit doing that.

And…something happened in his face. The carved-in-granite look softened. His eyes weren't quite so icy cold. "Go ahead, Mel," he said, almost gently. "Say it."

Her face got hot and her eyes were burning with tears she refused to let fall. Her racing heart seemed to stop. A ridiculous little bark of a cough escaped her. "Mel. You just called me Mel."

One side of his mouth quirked up. "Talk."

Hope. This was hope. Filling her heart. Making it beat again. "Well, ahem. As you know, I came to Bronco as an interim stop in my life."

"I am aware," he said quietly in that deep, rich voice she loved.

Her mind went blank. She blinked and shook her head and ordered her brain to get back online. "It, um, just never occurred to me that I might fall deeply in love. After the disaster of epic proportions that was Todd, I was so…anti-love. He was a cheater. I had *chosen* a cheater. I realized I couldn't trust my own judgment. I decided the best course was not to give any guy a chance. I never imagined I would end up with the possibility of real happiness staring me right in the face—and Gabe, I can't believe I was such a thoughtless fool, I really can't. I can't believe I called making love with you rebound sex. I can't believe I freaked and ran when you tried to tell me how you felt about me. I'm an idiot, I know it. But I *can* learn. I really can. And I *have* learned. I've, um, learned that it's *you*, Gabe. You're everything to me. I love you. I do. I was so stupid and wounded and blind. I only hope it's not too late."

He dropped his hat and took her by the shoulders. "Mel." His eyes—they were summer-day blue again. "Mel." It was all he seemed to be able to say. And it was more than enough.

Especially when he gathered her close and lowered his beautiful mouth to hers in a long, searching, perfect kiss.

She melted into him, there beneath the clear sky, by the rushing creek, in the very spot where they had first met.

When he lifted his head, he asked gruffly, "Does this mean you're going to let me say it now?"

She nodded up at him, a tear escaping, gliding along her temple and into her hair. "Please. Yes. Say it now."

He cradled her face in his big, rough hands. "I love you, Mel. You're my one. My only. There never was another. My whole life, I've been waiting. Just for you."

"Oh, Gabe." Now she was crying and laughing at the same time. "Oh, Gabe, I'm so glad. I was so afraid I'd lost you. I… I love you. I really, really do."

He laughed then, a rich, joyous sound. And then he captured her lips again and kissed her slow and deep.

When he lifted his head that time, he said, "Let's go." He bent and scooped up his hat. Rising again, he wrapped an arm across her shoulders. They headed up the hill, kissing as they went.

When they reached the vehicles, they stood at his driver's door for a half hour or so, holding each other, kissing each other, whispering promises they both knew now they were bound to keep.

"You work tonight?" he asked eventually.

"I'm on at five, yes."

"Follow me to my house now?"

"Yes." She grabbed his gorgeous face between her hands. "Yes, yes, yes!"

At Gabe's, after Mel took a minute to greet Butch properly, they went on to the master bedroom where they stayed for an hour and a half, celebrating their love in the most elemental way.

Later, they took Butch for a walk. George must have spotted them from the main house. He came running out—to say hi to Mel, he said. He'd read the diary and declared himself one hundred percent certain that Gramps had written it. He was all fired up to make plans to find out what had happened to Beatrix.

"We're on it," promised Gabe.

"Good, then. I was going to let your grandfather read the diary, if that's all right."

"That's fine," said Gabe. "Then we'll talk about the next step."

"That'll work." George tipped his hat at Mel. "Good to see you, Mel. Drop by the main house for dinner soon, won't you?"

"I will, definitely," she promised.

"Excellent." With a nod, George headed off in the direction of the stables.

Back at Gabe's house, Mel shared what

had happened during her visit to Rust Creek Falls.

Gabe said he understood her reluctance to approach Winona about the diary until they could learn more about the lost Beatrix.

"As for Todd," he added, "I would love to rearrange his face for him, but he's paying for being a cheating fool. He lost *you*—and his loss is the best thing that ever happened to me."

"Oh, I do love you," she whispered, lifting her eager mouth to welcome his kiss.

At four, she had to return to her apartment to get ready for work.

That night, Gabe showed up at closing time. He followed her to her place and slept over. In the morning, they spoke of the future. Mel would be going to work for DJ's as CFO. For now, she would keep her apartment.

But they both agreed she would be moving in with him at the Ambling A sometime in the next few months. Stark naked, he got down on one knee and officially asked her to marry him.

She couldn't say yes fast enough. Laughing with happiness, she threw herself into his arms.

Gabe said his grandfather had read the diary. Alexander was as eager as George to get going on the search for Beatrix.

Mel had an idea. "Amanda is amazing. She can find just about anyone or anything online. I was thinking we might hire her, give her the diary and what information we have, see what she can discover about what happened to Beatrix."

Gabe agreed. "It's a shot. Let's talk to her, see if she's up for playing online detective."

"That sounds good."

"And I was also thinking we should have a look up in the attic of the main house. There are years' worth of documents and keepsakes stored up there in trunks and dusty boxes. Might be something about Beatrix somewhere in all that stuff."

That night, when he showed up at DJ's,

Gabe brought the diary with him. He also reported that he, his dad and his mom had spent several hours in the attic of the main ranch house searching for clues to the mystery.

"So far, nothing," he said glumly.

She longed to grab him and kiss him— but the kisses would have to wait until after work. She folded her arms across her middle to keep them from reaching for him. "It's good that you looked, though. We need to follow every possible lead. Something is bound to turn up, eventually."

He grinned at her. "I do like your attitude lately."

She laughed with sheer happiness. "Must be love giving me a whole new outlook on life."

Monday morning, they knocked on Amanda's door. She was all smiles just to see them together. She offered coffee and they told her the story of Josiah and Winona and their lost child.

Amanda had tears in her eyes when the

story was through. She said of course she would help. "I'll find out what I can."

Later that day, back in Mel's apartment, as they sat at her little table eating ham and cheese sandwiches, Mel asked if Gabe would take her to Snowy Mountain Senior Care. "We need to tell Josiah that we're together now, that we'll be married. I just feel that he should know."

"I think he would like that." Gabe pushed his empty plate away. "I didn't tell you before, but that day he said to bring you to him, he also said that I shouldn't give up on love."

Mel got up and went to his side of the table. He pushed his chair back so that she could sit on his lap. She rested her head on his shoulder. "Your great-grandfather is a very wise man. Thank you for giving me a second chance."

Gabe stroked her hair and whispered, "I love you, Mel. You're mine and I am yours. I'm so damn glad you came back to me."

* * *

In his small living room at Snowy Mountain Senior Care, Josiah sat in his recliner. He stared blankly into space as Gabe explained that he had found the only woman for him.

Gabe took Mel's hand. "I told you, when it comes to Mel, I didn't have to ask. And I don't, Gramps. I knew from the first."

Mel admitted, "I wasn't so quick on the uptake, Josiah. I've had my heart broken and that made me wary and reluctant to give my trust. I was a fool. I almost ruined everything. But I finally saw the light. Gabe gave me another chance and, well, here we are. Together."

"Forever," added Gabe.

"And always," said Mel.

Josiah said nothing. He stared at the far wall.

Mel and Gabe got up and went around the coffee table to hug him.

"We'll be getting married," said Gabe.

"And Thursday, on Mel's next day off, I'm taking her to choose the ring."

Mel kissed the old man's wrinkled cheek. "Tonight, we'll tell George, Angela, Alexander and Malone that we're engaged."

Gabe laughed. "Mom will be so happy." He asked Mel, "Ice water?"

"I would love a glass."

He got their drinks and they sat across from the silent, unmoving old man. Mel talked about the new job she would be taking with DJ. Gabe said he was still working on Erica to come for a long visit home.

When they were ready to go, they carried their glasses to the sink and returned to the sitting area long enough to give Josiah one last hug.

They'd both reached the door when the old man spoke from behind them in his gruff, rusty voice. "Glad to see you two together where you belong. Now find my little girl."

Mel and Gabe turned in unison. "Oh, Josiah," Mel whispered, her eyes blurred with sudden tears.

Across the room, the old man sat, staring straight ahead, still as a statue again.

Gabe was shaken to the core. Gramps had just all but admitted that he and the Josiah of the diary were one and the same. He let the realization sink in and then spoke with calm assurance. "We promise you, Gramps. One way or another, we will find your little girl."

* * * * *

LET'S TALK

Romance

For exclusive extracts, competitions and special offers, find us online:

f facebook.com/millsandboon

⊙ @millsandboonuk

🐦 @millsandboon

Or get in touch on 0844 844 1351*

For all the latest titles coming soon, visit millsandboon.co.uk/nextmonth

Want even more
ROMANCE?

Join our bookclub today!